D0898906

The Man who fell in Love
with his Wife

by the same author

ALPHA BETA
THE FOURSOME
THE SEA ANCHOR
OLD FLAMES
MECCA

The Man who fell in Love with his Wife

Ted Whitehead

faber and faber
LONDON·BOSTON

First published in 1984
by Faber and Faber Limited
3 Queen Square London WC1N 3AU
Filmset by Wilmaset, Birkenhead
Printed in Great Britain by
Whitstable Litho Ltd Whitstable Kent
All rights reserved

© *Ted Whitehead, 1984*

British Library Cataloguing in Publication Data

Whitehead, Ted
The man who fell in love with his wife.
I. Title
822'.914   PR6073.H/

ISBN 0-571-13376-2

For Ann Chamberlain

The Man Who Fell in Love with His Wife derives from the author's BBC TV play *Sweet Nothings*, which was transmitted in 1980 and has been extensively rewritten for the stage.

The first stage production was at the Lyric Studio, Lyric Theatre, Hammersmith, on 27 February 1984 by arrangement with H. M. Tennent.

ACT ONE

Before the lights go up, music: 'Only you', sung by the Platters.

The scene is a lounge in a suburban house. Tidy, comfortable, a bit dull. Music centre. Television set, recorder. Couch. A bookcase, spilling over. A sideboard on which stands a statuette of the Madonna and Child.

Left, hallway and staircase. Right, door to kitchen (off).

MARY, *dressed neatly but anonymously, sits reading some Civil Service documents. Her daughter,* SUSY, *sits working on an essay. The scene is quiet, peaceful, industrious. It is a Sunday afternoon in August.*

TOM *looks out from the kitchen. He is a fit, strong-looking man nearing 40. Holds a can of beer and a glass. He surveys his domain for a moment in silence.*

TOM: Finish your papers in five minutes, please.
> (SUSY *laughs.*)
> I don't want to distract you but the match is on the box in five minutes.

SUSY: I'm going to meet Nick anyway.

MARY: And I'm nearly through.
> (TOM *glances at Mary's notes.*)

TOM: There's two M's in 'accommodation'.

MARY: Oh, help.

TOM: Well, you've survived the first week . . .

MARY: Yes.

TOM: I told you the job would be a doddle.

MARY: Mmmmm.

TOM: (*Laughs.*) You were in a terrible state last Monday!

MARY: I was nervous . . .

TOM: (*To* SUSY) When I dropped her outside the office she looked petrified!

SUSY: If you went back to work after twenty years of being a housewife, wouldn't you be nervous?

TOM: Yeah . . . especially on the docks!

MARY: How did your week go?

TOM: Oh, usual problems. Late cargoes, union troubles and

11

marriage breakdowns.

MARY: Marriage breakdowns?

TOM: Yes, I had this docker in the office, crying his eyes out.

MARY: Why?

TOM: His wife had walked out and left him with the kids. He didn't know what to do. Drinking himself legless.

MARY: What did you say?

TOM: I told him he should have given her a fourpenny one.

SUSY: Oh Dad!

TOM: Twenty-three years of age and he's got four kids. The dockers call him Phil . . . Phil the pram! They call his wife Marge. Marge, easy to . . . oh, you know what they're like.

SUSY: Why did his wife leave?

TOM: He said she'd been suffering from depression since she had the last child. Four kids! If he carries on like that he'll be able to give up work and live off the welfare. He'll be on your books, Mary.

SUSY: I suppose he's a Catholic.

TOM: Yeah, but I didn't have four kids, did I? One was quite enough.

SUSY: Thank you!

TOM: Nothing personal.

SUSY: Actually, Dad . . . I might be out of your way next year.

TOM: Getting married or something?

SUSY: I mean, I've got the chance of sharing a flat next term.

TOM: A flat? Where?

SUSY: Toxteth.

TOM: Bit rough round there. If you see a cat with its tail on, you know it's a tourist.

SUSY: Snob! It's a great area . . . lots of students live there.

TOM: Has it got an inside lavatory?

SUSY: All mod cons. Do you mind?

TOM: Mind? No, it's a good idea, love. Your mother and me deserve a bit of peace.

(SUSY *looks apprehensively at* MARY.)

MARY: Who will you be sharing with?

SUSY: Linda and Sally . . . and a couple of others.

TOM: A commune!

SUSY: Sort of . . .

TOM: If you're gonna live in a commune you're gonna need a big trunk with double locks.

SUSY: I'll leave my valuables here.

TOM: I mean for your bread and butter.

MARY: Will it be all girls?

SUSY: That's the plan.

TOM: St Trinians in Toxteth! Maybe I should join you. You'll need a man around.

MARY: Tom, be serious.

TOM: I'm being serious.

MARY: Won't it be very expensive?

SUSY: I'll get a rent allowance.

MARY: You haven't committed yourself, have you?

SUSY: No, not yet.

MARY: I think we ought to discuss it.

SUSY: Well, that was why I brought it up.

(SUSY *collects her things and goes upstairs.*)

MARY: It can be very difficult sharing a flat.

TOM: How would you know?

MARY: I shared with you.

TOM: When we got married.

MARY: Yes.

TOM: Oh, it was difficult, was it?

MARY: I don't know if it's a good idea.

TOM: She'll be all right.

MARY: There doesn't seem much point.

TOM: Well, she needs somewhere to study.

MARY: What's wrong with the spare room?

TOM: It's not the same, is it?

MARY: You could fix it up for her.

TOM: It's not the same thing.

(TOM *switches on the television.*)

I was gonna put a fiver on the Reds . . .

(TOM *goes to the kitchen for another beer.* MARY *goes upstairs.* TOM *carries on speaking.*)

Know what odds they offered? Two to one on! That's the problem . . .

13

(TOM *comes back with his beer. Surprised that* MARY *has gone.*)
You can never get decent odds on the Reds.
(TOM *looks at the television. Hears a thump from upstairs. Looks up. Another thump. Looks again, puzzled.* MARY *comes down in an underslip. Looks at* TOM, *smiles, embarrassed.*)
What are you doing?

MARY: Exercises.
(MARY *takes a sheet of paper from her file of documents.* TOM *plucks it away.*)

TOM: Exercises?

MARY: I'm completely out of shape.

TOM: Are you training for Miss World or what? (*Reads*) 'Legs . . . Waist . . . Bum.' You've got a lovely bum!
(TOM *touches her.*)

MARY: Stop.

TOM: 'Breasts'. What's wrong with your breasts?
(TOM *touches her.*)

MARY: Tom, don't. Give me the sheet.

TOM: Lovely!
(TOM *gives it to her. She goes to the stairs.* TOM *follows.*)

MARY: I want to do the exercises. I've got to buy a dress for the party next week . . . and I couldn't get into anything!

TOM: You've never worried about your figure before, you've got a great figure.

MARY: I was always a twelve—ever since we got married I was a twelve—now I'm almost a fourteen. I've got to exercise.

TOM: I could do with some exercise myself. Come here!
(TOM *seizes her with mock passion.* MARY *smiles, responds in the same mood.* TOM *pulls back hastily.*)
Hey up! I'm missing the match!
(MARY *pulls a face, goes upstairs.* TOM *hurries back to the television and sits with his drink.* SUSY *comes downstairs and looks in on her way out.*)

SUSY: Bye Dad, hope they win.

TOM: They will.

SUSY: Bye.

TOM: Bye bye, love.
(SUSY *goes.* TOM *glances after her for a second. Sings line of Beatles'*

14

song) 'She's leaving home, bye bye . . .'
(*Lights fade to blackout.*)

Lights up: Mid-evening on the following Friday. Empty lounge.
SUSY *comes downstairs. Looks for her bag. Checks this. Takes out a make-up bag. Looks inside, smiles, goes back upstairs.*
Sound of SUSY *and* MARY *laughing.*
Sound of TOM *calling* MARY *and knocking at door upstairs. The laughter stops.*
TOM *comes downstairs, wearing a greenish shirt and fawn trousers. Carries a brown tie.*

TOM: Hurry up in there!
   (TOM *goes to a mirror and starts knotting the tie.* SUSY *comes downstairs.*)
   Hasn't fallen in, has she? What are you doing?
SUSY: Helping Mum with the fake . . .
TOM: Eh?
SUSY: The warpaint.
   (TOM *puts on his jacket.*)
TOM: It would be tonight, wouldn't it, this bloody do . . . with England playing at Wembley.
SUSY: Is it on the box?
TOM: Aye.
SUSY: I'll tape it for you.
TOM: I'll know the result though, won't I? Somebody's bound to tell me the result. (*Goes to the stairs.*) We're gonna be late . . .
SUSY: Wait.
TOM: What?
SUSY: Don't go up yet.
TOM: Why not?
SUSY: Let her finish off . . .
TOM: She's been ages in there.
SUSY: She's nearly ready.
TOM: I hate being late.
SUSY: You won't know her, Dad. Have a drink.
TOM: By the time we get to this leaving do everyone will have left.

15

(SUSY *hurries back upstairs.* TOM *goes into the kitchen. Returns with a Scotch. Looks at himself in the mirror. Brushes his coat. Calls*)

Mary, it's half-eight. Hurry up.

(*No response.* TOM *goes to the stairs.*)

Come on, Mary, shake a leg!

(*Indistinct reply from upstairs.*)

Look, if we've got to go to this party . . .

(MARY *comes down the stairs. Stops half-way.* SUSY *comes behind her, smiling.*)

MARY: Sorry, I won't be a sec.

(TOM *looks up at* MARY. *He's genuinely surprised. An illumination.* MARY *is wearing fifties-style clothes—a tight lowcut dress with box shoulders and slit skirt. High-heeled shoes. New hairstyle. She looks anxiously at* TOM.)

Do I look all right? How do I look?

(TOM *wolf-whistles.* MARY *smiles. Plucks at the slit skirt.*)

It doesn't look funny, does it?

TOM: Sensational.

(MARY *comes downstairs, followed by* SUSY.)

SUSY: What did I tell you?

TOM: Going out without your underslip on!

MARY: It's the style now . . . all the fifties gear . . .

TOM: I haven't forgotten, you know. You look 16 again.

MARY: Sixteen plus wrinkles.

SUSY: Don't her eyes look lovely?

TOM: Yeah . . . what have you done to them?

SUSY: I used a kohl stick.

TOM: Coal?

SUSY: Kohl! K–o–h–l.

MARY: It's a pencil. I've never used it before.

TOM: Don't tell me the secrets, you'll spoil it.

MARY: Does it look all right?

TOM: Very glamorous!

MARY: Oh, aye. (*Turns back to the stairs.*) Susy, could you—

TOM: Hang on.

MARY: Uh?

TOM: What about me?

MARY: What?

TOM: How do I look?
> (TOM *displays his suit.* MARY *looks him up and down.*)
MARY: You'll do.
TOM: Oh, thanks!
MARY: I won't be long.
TOM: Hey, I've got an idea.
MARY: What?
TOM: About this leaving do.
MARY: Mmm?
TOM: Let's skip it and stay in!
> (TOM *seizes* MARY.)
MARY: Tom, I've got to go . . .
TOM: Give us a kiss!
MARY: (*Resisting*) Tom . . .
TOM: Remember our first date? (*Then to* SUSY) I tried to kiss her then and she wouldn't let me.
MARY: Nice girls didn't, then.
> (MARY *frees herself.* TOM *pecks at her face but she turns aside.*)
> Tom, my make-up! Let me finish getting ready. Susy . . .
> (MARY *goes up the stairs and* SUSY *follows.* TOM *looks up after them.*)
SUSY: Just a spray of glitter, Mum . . . and you'll really knock them out!
> (TOM *stands at the bottom of the stairs for a moment, the tiny rejection bothering him. Lights fade to blackout.*)

Lights up: A few hours later, after midnight.

> SUSY *sits reading and taking notes. Door bangs.* TOM *comes in, from the hall by the stairs.*
SUSY: (*Smiling*) Dirty stopouts!
> (TOM *goes toward the kitchen.*)
> How was the do?
> (TOM *goes into the kitchen.* SUSY *looks after him, puzzled.* MARY *comes in. She's a bit tipsy, sways.*)
> How was it?
MARY: Great . . .

SUSY: Did they like your style?

MARY: Oh yes . . . (*Giggles.*) I was . . . the belle of the ball!

SUSY: There's some fresh coffee . . .

(SUSY *half stands.* MARY *goes past her.*)

MARY: S'all right.

(MARY *goes toward the kitchen and almost bangs into* TOM *as he comes out. He stands aside with excessive courtesy.*)

Oops!

(MARY *goes into the kitchen.* TOM *comes into the lounge with a glass of Scotch.*)

SUSY: I taped the game, Dad.

(TOM *nods, drinks.*)

It was a great game. You'll love it!

TOM: You mean they won?

SUSY: (*Dismayed*) Didn't you know?

(TOM *shakes his head. Silence.*)

Mum seems to have enjoyed herself.

TOM: Aye.

SUSY: What was it like . . . the do?

TOM: Disco. Drinks.

SUSY: Did you have a dance?

TOM: Yeah, I had a couple of dances. Your mother was never off the floor.

SUSY: My mum!

TOM: Aye.

SUSY: Is she that popular?

TOM: Oh aye. In great demand.

SUSY: What were they like? The office crowd?

(MARY *comes back with a coffee. Stands.*)

TOM: Young.

SUSY: Young?

TOM: Aye. Young crowd.

MARY: Well, what did you expect?

TOM: Greybeards.

MARY: What?

TOM: I thought all Civil Servants were greybeards.

MARY: (*Laughs.*) Oh Tom!

(SUSY *looks from* MARY *to* TOM. *Both are still standing, as if waiting for each other either to sit or go upstairs.* SUSY *collects the rest of her notes.*)

SUSY: Think I'll hit the pit.

(SUSY *goes upstairs.* TOM *stares at* MARY.)

TOM: What are you after then? Promotion?

MARY: (*Smiling*) What?

— TOM: You were dancing with him all night.

MARY: Who?

TOM: The boss.

MARY: Bob Reece?

TOM: You haven't forgotten who the boss is, have you?

MARY: Bob's not the boss.

TOM: Isn't he?

MARY: No.

TOM: What is he then?

MARY: He's an HEO.

TOM: A what?

MARY: A Higher Executive Officer.

(MARY *is amused,* TOM *wild but trying to control it.*)

Above him is an SEO.

TOM: Eh?

MARY: A Senior Executive Officer. And below him is an EO. And below the EO is a CO. Clerical Officer. Me!

(MARY *looks at* TOM, *goes toward him. He doesn't respond.*)

And below me . . .

TOM: Skip it.

MARY: Believe it or not there is a grade below me.

TOM: I don't want the whole bloody hierarchy.

MARY: A CA. A Clerical Assistant.

TOM: You were dancing with him all night.

MARY: I wasn't.

TOM: You were.

MARY: I wasn't.

TOM: You couldn't take your eyes off him all night.

MARY: I wasn't. I didn't.

TOM: Your eyes were on stalks! When you weren't dancing with him you were following him around.

MARY: And were you following me?

19

TOM: All you were interested in was chatting him up.

MARY: I was with you. I danced with you.

TOM: Yeah, twice!

MARY: You don't like dancing.

TOM: Oh, was that it?

MARY: I was dancing with you till Julia cut in.

TOM: Did you arrange that?

MARY: No!

TOM: And then you went and got him up to dance. You went and asked him up.

MARY: Well, there's nothing wrong with that, is there?

TOM: Julia was amazed. Said she'd never seen him dance with anyone before. She thought he didn't like dancing.

MARY: Huh, I don't think he does! He's so awkward. You saw him . . .

TOM: I see. You didn't dance with me because I don't like dancing. Instead, you danced with him because he doesn't like dancing.

MARY: Why are you twisting everything?

TOM: I'm not twisting anything! I'm saying what happened. You left me with Julia and you went and asked Bob Reece to dance. Why? Have you got a soft spot for him?

MARY: No . . .

TOM: Did you feel sorry for him? Standing there all on his own . . . with his big sad eyes, spaniel eyes . . . which were locked into yours!

MARY: I'm going to bed.

(MARY *turns away.* TOM *confronts her.*)

TOM: Hang on.

MARY: What?

TOM: Let's get this straight.

(MARY *waits.*)

You made it pretty obvious, didn't you?

MARY: Made what obvious?

TOM: That you fancied him.

MARY: Tom . . .

(MARY *looks at him incredulously.*)

TOM: You made it obvious there. I'll give you that. You didn't

20

try to disguise it. Were you trying to tell me?

MARY: Tom . . .

TOM: Admit it.

MARY: Tom, all I have to tell you is that you're completely wrong about Bob . . . and you've had too much to drink. You'll laugh at yourself tomorrow. Have some coffee . . .

TOM: I don't want any coffee, thanks.

MARY: Well I do. (*Studies* TOM. *Smiles.*) Tom Fearon . . .

TOM: What?

MARY: I've always known you had a wild imagination but tonight . . . tonight you're surpassing yourself!

TOM: Am I?

MARY: I don't give a damn about anyone else in the world except you. Isn't that obvious? Isn't that what I make obvious? I mean . . . I'm embarrassed by what I feel for you. It hardly seems decent.

TOM: Huh . . .

MARY: It hurts me when you say things like . . . like tonight. You've known me for twenty-odd years . . . have I ever given you cause, any cause . . . ?
(MARY *suddenly a little tearful.* TOM *looks away.*)
I'm sorry if I hurt you but . . . Look, Tom. When I first went into that office my knees were shaking. I was terrified. And Bob helped me. He was kind. He's a really kind, gentle man. Very shy . . .

TOM: Uh.

MARY: It never crossed my mind that you might be . . . jealous . . . of Bob! Anyway, most of the time we were talking about you. He liked you.

TOM: Did he?

MARY: Yes, he did. And you'd like him, if you knew him. I hope you do know him. I mean I hope you get to know him.
(*Goes into the kitchen. Calls*) Have some coffee.
(TOM *doesn't reply. Picks up his drink. Puts it down again.*)

TOM: You didn't fancy him then?

MARY: (*Calls*) Actually it was Bob who fancied me.

TOM: Oh did he?
(MARY *comes back with two cups of coffee. Goes to* TOM.)

MARY: Yes, when he saw me tonight he gasped and said: 'My God, Mary, I never realized how beautiful you were!' And when we were dancing he put his arms around me and whispered in my ear: 'Play your cards right, girl, and one day I'll make you an EO.'

TOM: A what?

MARY: An Executive Officer.

(MARY *laughs.* TOM *is sullen and uncertain.* MARY *leans forward to kiss him but he pushes her away violently. The coffee spills.* MARY *stares at* TOM, *shocked.* TOM *goes and gets his Scotch.*)

What's the matter with you? I've never seen you like this before.

TOM: You've never treated me like that before.

MARY: How?

TOM: You virtually ignored me all night!

MARY: I did not!

TOM: You walked right past me at one point and didn't even see me.

MARY: When?

TOM: You brushed my arm and didn't even notice me.

MARY: When was this?

TOM: You and Bob Reece were saying goodnight to some of the crowd. And when you came back in you walked right past me!

MARY: Well, I'm sorry. If I did, it wasn't intentional.

TOM: That's what hurt.

MARY: I didn't mean to hurt you . . .

TOM: You were just too absorbed in following Reece . . . Mr Reece . . . all over the place.

MARY: I was not!

TOM: Couldn't you have waited till Monday?

MARY: Actually—

TOM: You'll have plenty of time with him on Monday, won't you?

MARY: Actually I don't know if I can face going in on Monday.

TOM: Oh? Why not?

MARY: You made me look ridiculous there.

TOM: *I* did?

MARY: Storming out like that when all I wanted was a last drink.

TOM: You'd had enough last drinks.

MARY: That's for me to decide.

TOM: Oh is it?

MARY: Why did you tell me to ask the boss for a lift? You made me look ridiculous in front of everyone.

TOM: You'd already made yourself look ridiculous. (*Mocks her dress.*) Look at yourself . . . the belle of the ball! Huh!

MARY: Actually . . . actually I feel like an old hen!

(MARY *rushes upstairs.* TOM *stands still for a second. Then goes to the bottom of the stairs. Listens. Goes up a couple of stairs. Stops. Hesitates. Comes back down. Goes to the sideboard where he had left his drink. Drains the glass. Sees Mary's brightly coloured scarf. Seizes it as if to tear it to pieces. Instead, lets it fall. Looks at a framed photograph of himself and Mary. Picks it up from the sideboard. Looks closely at it. Puts it back. He turns towards the stairs again. Hesitates. Then takes his glass into the kitchen. Comes back with the glass full. Sits down. Goes to the sideboard. Opens a drawer and rummages in it. Can't find what he wants. Kneels to open bottom drawer. For a second, kneeling, he looks up at the statuette of the Madonna and Child. Takes an album of photographs from the drawer. The cover is worn and old. Opens the album and glances through it. Puts a tape on the music centre: Nat King Cole singing 'Unforgettable'. Sits with his drink and studies the album. After a moment* MARY *comes quietly down the stairs. She's wearing a nightdress. Near the bottom of the staircase she stops and looks at* TOM, *who is absorbed.* TOM *looks up. Sees her. Stands. Goes to the staircase.* MARY *comes down to him. Embraces him.*)

What are you doing?

TOM: I was just . . .

(TOM *can't speak.* MARY *draws him back to the chair. He sits. She perches on the arm.*)

MARY: Tom it's all right, it's all right . . .

TOM: I was just reminding myself . . . (*Opens the album.*) Oh, it's . . . fatal!

MARY: What?

TOM: Looking at old albums . . .

MARY: Listening to old songs . . .

TOM: Yeah.

23

MARY: Pure sentimentality.

TOM: Yeah.

(TOM *closes the album.*)

MARY: I love it.

(MARY *kisses him. Opens the album.*)

Look at you there! The state of you . . . with your D.A. hairstyle!

TOM: All the rage then.

MARY: I haven't forgotten . . .

TOM: Head full of margarine!

MARY: Now they use gel.

TOM: Look at that one . . . the Cock o' the North!

MARY: How old were you then?

TOM: About 14.

MARY: Who took the snap.

TOM: Dunno . . . some girlfriend, I suppose.

MARY: You don't remember who?

TOM: No . . . all the faces blur.

MARY: Huh! The state of you there . . . in your duffle coat.

TOM: Once I put that on I felt like the Brain of Britain. Wore it all the time. Always had a paperback sticking out of the pocket, like . . .

MARY: I remember. You had that coat for ages. What happened to it?

TOM: It got nicked one day in the sandhills . . . at Freshfield, when we were having a swim. You lost a handbag. Remember?

MARY: Oh yes . . . Hey, get me there!

TOM: All white face and black hollow eyes!

MARY: That was my beatnik period.

TOM: How old were you then?

MARY: About . . . 15.

TOM: Who took the photie?

MARY: A boyfriend.

TOM: I thought you didn't have any boyfriends?

MARY: Only one.

TOM: Who?

MARY: You.

TOM: Me? Did I take this?

MARY: Yes. Good, isn't it?

TOM: My memory's going.

MARY: Tom, it was twenty years ago.

TOM: And more.

MARY: Don't remind me. You know, I think that's the earliest photograph of me I've got. There might be a school photo somewhere . . . but I don't think I've got any snaps from before I met you.

TOM: Well, they wouldn't be worth keeping, would they?

MARY: No.

TOM: Here's one of us queuing up outside the Cavern Club.

MARY: Queuing up for modern jazz!

TOM: Real intellectuals, weren't we?

MARY: Well, the Beatles were still in Hamburg then.

TOM: Where's this?

MARY: Otterspool.

TOM: Oh aye, Otterspool Promenade. The Iron Coast! All the junk . . . Romantic, isn't it?

MARY: It seemed the height of romance to me twenty years ago.

TOM: We always used to shoot out there at lunchtime.

MARY: Yes . . . and sit and look at the river . . . holding hands and feeding each other fish and chips.

TOM: They've cleaned it all up now. Hey, now you're working in town, we'll be able to shoot out there again at lunchtime.

MARY: I thought you always stayed at the docks?

TOM: Oh, I don't have to. We'll shoot out there again.

MARY: Right. Fish and chips, the Mersey and you . . . Paradise!
(TOM *kisses her*.)

TOM: Hey . . .

MARY: What? What's wrong?

TOM: You taste of fish and chips.

MARY: So do you.

TOM: Lovely!
(*Lights fade to blackout*.)

Lights up: Afternoon, a week later. Bright sunshine. Lounge empty. Some parcels on the settee.

25

SUSY *comes in from the hall, wearing a tatty anorak and jeans. Goes straight to the bookcase. Takes out a file and looks in it. Puts it back. Takes out a folder containing handwritten essays. Looks through these. Finds the one she wants. Puts it back in the folder and leaves this on top of the bookcase. Goes to the kitchen, taking off the anorak.*

After a moment MARY *comes down the stairs, dressed in frilly lingerie with black stockings and suspender belt. Her hair tumbles free, and she's flushed and smiling. She goes to the parcels. Takes out a diaphanous slip. Smiles broadly. Looks up as* TOM *calls from upstairs.*

TOM: (*Calls*) Come on Mary! Hurry up! Mary!

> (MARY *looks through the parcels.* SUSY *comes from the kitchen, carrying a glass of orange juice. Stares in astonishment at* MARY. MARY *turns, sees her, freezes.*)

SUSY: (*Smiles*) Mum. . . !

> (MARY *gasps. Drops the slip. Runs upstairs.* SUSY *laughs and goes to the parcels. Takes out various bits of frilly underwear. Holds them up.* TOM *comes downstairs, wearing a dressing-gown.*)

TOM: Hello hello.

SUSY: Hello hello!

TOM: I thought you had a tutorial today?

SUSY: (*Laughing*) I forgot my essay.

TOM: Have you got it?

SUSY: Yes.

TOM: Well, are you going then, or what?

SUSY: What are you and Mum doing?

TOM: What do you think?

SUSY: She looks very nice.

TOM: Go on, get your essay.

SUSY: Sorry if I interrupted.

TOM: That's all right. Come on.

SUSY: Aren't you working today?

TOM: We went to Otterspool and then decided to have an afternoon off.

SUSY: Shopping . . .

TOM: Yeah. Come on, Susy.

> (SUSY *holds up a suspender belt.*)

SUSY: I like it!

(TOM *takes the belt and stretches it, aiming it at* SUSY *like a catapult.*)

TOM: You'll like it in the gob if you don't get a move on.

SUSY: It's not worth going to the tutorial now.

TOM: Well, go the library, or go the pictures, go anywhere . . . I'll give you the money.

SUSY: OK, I'll make myself scarce.

(SUSY *goes to the kitchen to get her anorak. Comes back, putting it on. She's highly tickled, keeps smiling.*)

Is it an anniversary or something?

TOM: Every day's an anniversary.

SUSY: What are you celebrating?

TOM: Us.

(SUSY *goes toward the hall. Stops.*)

SUSY: Will it be all right if I come back tonight?

TOM: Go on! Beat it!

(*They laugh.* SUSY *goes.* TOM *starts up the stairs.* MARY *comes down and meets him half-way. She has put a dress on.*)

She's gone.

MARY: I know. I heard her go. God, I got a shock when I saw her!

TOM: I bet she got more of a shock when she saw you.

MARY: Don't! I'd rather forget it.

(MARY *starts down.* TOM *blocks the way.*)

TOM: I still feel frisky.

MARY: Yes, well, I feel exhausted. I need a drink.

TOM: Get me one, will you?

(TOM *goes upstairs.* MARY *comes down. Stuffs the lingerie into the parcels. Goes into the kitchen.* TOM *comes down carrying a Polaroid camera, and several snaps. Looks at these, laughing.* MARY *comes in with two glasses of Scotch.*)

These are terrific!

MARY: Mmm . . . where are we going to put them?

TOM: We could put them round the walls.

MARY: Oh sure! The neighbours would love that!

TOM: They'd be dead jealous. Hey, Mary one more snap.

MARY: Haven't we got enough?

TOM: No, I mean . . . just one . . . You with the dress on.

MARY: It'll be a change.

TOM: Come on then, show a leg.

(MARY *poses like a glamour model.*)

That's right . . . lift your skirt a bit there . . . put your leg up on the chair.

(MARY *stands with her leg on the chair.* TOM *comes over and takes a shot up the dress.* MARY *laughs, jumps away.*)

MARY: I don't know how I'll face Susy.

TOM: She was made up!

MARY: Huh?

TOM: She was. She was tickled pink. She'll be boasting to all her mates.

MARY: Tom, don't.

TOM: She didn't know the old folks could be so frisky. It was a revelation.

MARY: Revelation to me too.

TOM: Nice one, though.

MARY: Oh, aye. What's the snap like?

(TOM *shows the Polaroid snap.*)

TOM: Oh, very saucy!

(MARY *looks at the shot and giggles.*)

MARY: Tom Fearon . . .

TOM: If Father Gallagher saw that, he'd send you to a nunnery.

MARY: And you to a monastery. Here . . . let me take one of you.

TOM: No naughties, now!

MARY: Just stand over there.

TOM: OK. How do you want me to look?

MARY: Manly.

TOM: That's no problem!

(TOM *adopts a Mr Universe pose and* MARY *takes the snap. Sits. They drink.*)

All right?

MARY: Yes.

TOM: Think of them all now, slaving away in the office.

MARY: Tom!

TOM: What?

MARY: You frighten me sometimes.

TOM: Me? Why?

MARY: You say just what I was going to say . . . or what I
    was thinking.

TOM: Well, you do the same with me.

MARY: Do I?

TOM: Sometimes.

MARY: We've been too long together!

TOM: Eh?

MARY: Well, it's a bit frightening, isn't it?

TOM: What?

MARY: Two people sharing their thoughts . . . their minds.

TOM: What's the snap like?

　　(MARY *shows the snap*.)

MARY: Very masculine.

TOM: Look at those muscles!

　　(*They sip their drinks*.)

MARY: I hope it will be all right at the office.

TOM: You said Julia would cover for you.

MARY: Yes, but . . . well, they are pretty busy in the office.

TOM: They don't know what life is about!

MARY: I wouldn't like to risk—

TOM: What's more important . . . me or work?

MARY: Oh, that's not fair!

TOM: You've got to get your priorities right.

MARY: What about you?

TOM: What?

MARY: You'll be missed at the docks.

TOM: Oh, they can spare me for one afternoon in twenty years.
    Give us a kiss.

　　(*They kiss*.)

MARY: Tom—will you tell me something . . . honestly?

TOM: (*Nuzzling*) Mmm . . . what?

MARY: There isn't anybody else—is there?

TOM: Anybody else?

MARY: Another woman?

TOM: Eh?

　　(TOM *laughs*.)

MARY: Is there?

　　(TOM *shakes his head, amused at the idea*.)

29

Tom . . . I'd rather know . . . if . . .

TOM: No.

MARY: I would rather know. Honestly.

TOM: There never has been anybody else. Never will be.

MARY: It's just that—oh, these last weeks . . . It doesn't matter.

TOM: You're funny.

MARY: Sorry.

TOM: Don't be sorry.

MARY: I love you.

TOM: I love you.

(*They kiss tenderly.* TOM *puts on a tape: 'Let's spend the night together' by the Rolling Stones.* TOM *sits with* MARY. *They kiss passionately.*)

MARY: Let's go upstairs.

TOM: No.

MARY: Tom!

TOM: What?

MARY: Don't.

TOM: Mmm?

MARY: Stop.

TOM: Mmmmmm.

MARY: Let's go upstairs.

TOM: No.

MARY: Come on.

TOM: Come here.

MARY: No.

TOM: What?

MARY: Tom . . .

TOM: Uh?

MARY: Tom . . . not here . . .

TOM: Lovely . . .

MARY: Let's go upstairs.

TOM: Don't want to.

MARY: Why not?

TOM: Wanna stay here.

MARY: We can't.

TOM: Uh?

MARY: Tom, we can't stay here.

TOM: Why not?

MARY: Susy'll be back.

TOM: No.

MARY: She will.

TOM: She won't.

MARY: Let's go upstairs.

TOM: No.

MARY: Why?

TOM: Not the same.

MARY: Oh . . . Tom!

TOM: (*Embracing her*) Don't you love me then?

MARY: Of course I do. You know I do.

TOM: I love you.

MARY: But Tom . . . (*Kisses him.*) Tom, please . . . can't we go upstairs?

TOM: No. Wanna stay here. Here. On the couch!

MARY: On the couch!

TOM: On the couch, Mary!

MARY: You're daft!

(TOM *draws her down.*)

TOM: Come on, Mary . . . On the couch!

MARY: Somebody might come in!

TOM: No they won't no they won't no they won't.

MARY: Tom Fearon!

TOM: Mmmm?

MARY: You'll get ten thousand Hail Marys for this.

TOM: Why? You're my wife, aren't you?

(*Lights fade to blackout.*)

Lights up: Early evening in September, two weeks later.

JULIA *stands near the sideboard. She is in her thirties and is wearing an outdoor coat and skirt. She looks curiously at the family photographs and at the Madonna statuette.*

SUSY *comes downstairs, dressed for a night out.*

SUSY: Hi, Julia.

JULIA: Hi. Where are you off?

SUSY: Gig at the Union.

JULIA: What are you studying?

31

SUSY: Humanities. It's a mixed bag . . . English and American
Lit., Women's Studies, History . . .
(JULIA *looks at the crammed bookcase.*)
JULIA: It's mixed all right. Alexandra Kollontai . . . Ernest
Hemingway . . . *Eve and the New Jerusalem*. I read that
recently. Marvellous book . . .
SUSY: Yes, I'm half-way through it. I've got to do an essay about
the pioneers of birth control in the nineteenth century.
JULIA: You've got to admire their guts, haven't you? Those early
radicals . . . preaching feminism and socialism when most
people were still stuck in the Middle Ages.
SUSY: Most people still are.
(JULIA *looks quizzically at* SUSY. MARY *comes from the kitchen,
carrying a paint roller. Gives it to* JULIA.)
MARY: Compliments of the house.
JULIA: The miracles of technology!
MARY: Take your coat off.
JULIA: I'd better make a move.
MARY: Well, have a quickie before you go.
JULIA: Another quickie?
MARY: I won't be seeing you for a week.
JULIA: I shall be desolate!
(MARY *goes back to the kitchen.*)
SUSY: Week off?
JULIA: Yes.
SUSY: What will you do? Any plans?
JULIA: Yes. Decorating!
(TOM *comes in from the hall, wearing a dark business suit and
raincoat.*)
TOM: I've been looking all over for you.
JULIA: Really?
TOM: I just missed you at the office. They said you'd gone to the
pub.
JULIA: Yes, we went to the Strand.
TOM: I just missed you at the Strand.
JULIA: We went on to the Grapes.
TOM: I went on to the Pig and Whistle.
JULIA: Why didn't you ring up and let us know?

TOM: Be easier if you'd stick to one pub.

JULIA: I'll propose it to the After-work Drinks Committee.

(MARY *comes in with drinks for herself and* JULIA. *Sees* TOM.)

MARY: Hello, love.

TOM: Hello.

MARY: Julia wanted to borrow the roller . . . You don't need it, do you?

TOM: You know I don't decorate in September. I decorate in spring.

JULIA: Very sensible, too.

TOM: What are you painting?

JULIA: The hallway in the flat. It's all green and cream. Like entering an institution.

MARY: Shall I put your pizza on, Tom?

TOM: No, I've got to dash out again.

MARY: Oh. Why?

TOM: See some docker.

MARY: Like a drink?

TOM: Ta.

(MARY *goes to the kitchen*.)

JULIA: Cheers.

TOM: How's the office?

JULIA: That's green and cream too.

TOM: Maybe you ought to repaint that.

JULIA: It would still be an institution.

TOM: Mary seems to like it.

JULIA: Mary has only been there a few weeks, Tom.

SUSY: How long have you been there?

JULIA: Since I left school, and don't ask me how long that is.

(SUSY *has picked up a book*. MARY *returns with the drink*.)

SUSY: What's the book, Mum?

MARY: A biography.

SUSY: Peter Handke. *A Sorrow Beyond Dreams*. German?

MARY: Yes.

JULIA: Austrian actually.

MARY: Oh . . .

SUSY: A biography of who?

33

MARY: His mother. He tries to see her not just as his mother . . .
but as a woman, and then not just as a woman but as a
human being.

SUSY: Interesting . . .

JULIA: You phoney, Mary!

MARY: What?

JULIA: That's exactly what Bob said when he lent it to me.

MARY: I suppose he says it to all the girls!

(MARY *and* JULIA *are convulsed, giggling.* TOM *looks on sourly.*
SUSY *puts the book away.*)

SUSY: What's your flat like, Julia?

JULIA: It's all right. It's got one huge room that I can organize
any way I like. That's the main thing. And there are a
couple of smaller rooms.

SUSY: All to yourself?

JULIA: Just little me.

SUSY: Sounds great.

TOM: Isn't it a bit lonely?

JULIA: Depends who I'm sharing with.

(SUSY *laughs.*)

Oh, I've tried all the arrangements and they all have
drawbacks.

(SUSY *looks at* JULIA *with curiosity.*)

Left my family because they kept grilling me about
marriage possibilities. No sooner got a flat on my own than
a man joined me and of course we did get married.

MARY: I didn't know you'd been married, Julia.

JULIA: We all have our skeletons . . . Got divorced, lived with a
group for a while, but I was the only smoker and they were
all health freaks. For a while I shared with a woman who
was always going on slimming kicks and eating all my
chocolates. When I ran out of places to hide them I moved
out. Actually went back and lived with Mummy for a
while.

TOM: And . . . Daddy?

JULIA: Oh no, he'd split by then. Mummy had served her time,
and boy, was she making up for it! I couldn't keep up with
her. Couldn't stand the pace. So I got my own flat . . . to

recuperate. Like I said, there are drawbacks to every
arrangement . . . but it's simpler if the chief drawback is
you . . . yourself.

(*They drink in silence.* SUSY *goes upstairs.*)

Bob's got a nice flat.

MARY: Has he?

JULIA: Yes. In Crosby. Marvellous view. Overlooking the river.

MARY: You've been there, have you?

JULIA: I went there one weekend to work on a report with him.
Don't tell the office.

MARY: Uh?

JULIA: You know what they're like.

TOM: What? What are they like?

JULIA: Oh, it's a hotbed of speculation.

TOM: Is it?

JULIA: Mr Dean and Miss Jayson have a drink every night after
work. But not with the rest of the crowd. No, they go to the
basement bar in the New Court pub . . . they've been
spotted! What are his intentions? Or her achievements? Mr
Andrews and his secretary, Mrs Alton, are always the last
to leave the office . . . yet neither is known for their
dedication to work. What is going on? Miss Casey has
applied for six months' leave of absence . . . why? A happy
event? Mr Smith stays in at lunchtime and locks his
door . . .

TOM: OK, OK . . .

JULIA: I suppose it makes typing bearable.

TOM: And do they gossip about Bob Reece?

JULIA: Well, as a bachelor in his thirties, I suppose Bob Reece is
a natural target for speculation.

TOM: What's he like?

JULIA: He's a lovely feller but a lousy writer.

(JULIA *and* MARY *laugh.*)

TOM: Eh?

JULIA: We have to vet his reports before they go for typing. You
should see his handwriting.

MARY: He's seen it.

TOM: Have I?

35

MARY: Those reports I was working on.
    (JULIA *takes a handwritten sheet from her bag.*)
JULIA: Read that.
TOM: (*Struggles to read.*) 'Incidence of . . . deliberate pregnancies in . . . unmarried girls . . .'
JULIA: You did well.
TOM: What's it about?
JULIA: 'Biology fights back'.
TOM: Uh?
JULIA: It seems that an increasing number of girls are deliberately getting pregnant because they can't find any jobs, and their boyfriends can't find any jobs, and they're both stuck with their parents, who want them out, so . . . so the girl gets pregnant and then she can claim a flat from the Corporation and financial support from us. We of course are not allowed to suggest abortion. So we pay up. And then we employ snoopers to make sure that the father is not actually cohabiting with the mother.
TOM: Crazy.
JULIA: Yes.
TOM: What a system.
JULIA: In the end, the girls end up with neither love nor work.
    (*Laughs.*) 'Lieben und arbeiten'.
MARY: (*Laughs.*) Huh . . . yes!
TOM: What?
JULIA: It's a sign that Bob keeps in his office. It's from Freud. Rules for the good life. 'Lieben und arbeiten'. 'Love and Work'.
TOM: I see.
MARY: Bob keeps it over his desk.
TOM: Does he keep it over his bed too? (*Glances at the report again. To* JULIA) M–s . . . Do you always use that title?
JULIA: Yes.
TOM: Why?
JULIA: Why not? I don't see that it's anyone's business whether I'm a Miss or a Mrs. So I use Ms.
TOM: But . . . it . . . it's unpronounceable.
MARY: She just pronounced it.

TOM: Why don't you want people to know you're not married?

MARY: That's not the point.

TOM: You don't call yourself Ms.

MARY: Only because I've got used to calling myself 'Mrs'. I mean, I'm not trying to advertise the fact that I'm married. It's . . . (MARY *drains her glass.*) It's just habit, isn't it?

TOM: What, marriage?

MARY: No, 'Mrs'!

JULIA: Look, Tom, you call yourself 'Mr Fearon', don't you?

TOM: Yeah.

JULIA: And nobody knows from that title whether you're married or not. So why women—

TOM: They do when they see the ring, don't they? That's why I wear it. I'm proud to be married and I want people to know.

MARY: Another drink?

TOM: I'm driving.

JULIA: And I'd better make a move.

MARY: Oh, have another.

(MARY *goes to kitchen.*)

JULIA: What's this then, Tom? Overtime?

TOM: I don't get overtime. No . . . I've got to see a docker who's got problems. His wife has left him with four kids, so he's farmed the kids out to various relatives and spends every night in the pub getting paralytic.

JULIA: He'll end up on our books.

TOM: Yeah . . . but he's still working, or . . . well, reporting for duty. Had to send him home last week. But he doesn't want to be home.

JULIA: I'm not surprised.

TOM: It's all down to money.

JULIA: Is it?

TOM: We get blokes at the docks producing sick notes for all sorts of things like, say, migraine, or stomach ache, or backache . . . all supposed to be physical problems. They're off work for a week or a month, or months on end. I think if the doctor could give them cash in the hand they'd be miraculously cured. You know, if the doctor could examine

37

him and say, 'You've got bad rheumatism, how about
five hundred quid?' and give the money on the spot. Say a
hundred for a headache and two-fifty for gastro-
enteritis . . . And the bloke could go straight back to work
with all his problems solved!
(MARY *has returned with the drinks*.)

JULIA: All the problems, Tom?

TOM: Well, most of them. I'd better go and see him. Sort him
out. Father Fearon! (*Goes to stairs*.) Susy? You want a lift
into town?

SUSY: (*Calls*) Right. Lovely!

TOM: You, Julia?

JULIA: No, it's all right, thanks, Tom. The bus drops me right at
the door.

TOM: Where's that?

JULIA: Princes Avenue.

TOM: Oh aye . . . in the red lights.

JULIA: Yes, a girl doesn't go short of propositions there. You
know, the women don't even take the men back to their
rooms now.

TOM: Maybe because the husband is in the room.

JULIA: Maybe. Anyway, they just do it al fresco.
(SUSY *comes down*.)

TOM: Reminds me of when we were courting.

MARY: Tom!

TOM: We were like that.

MARY: We were not.
(TOM *smiles at* JULIA *and* SUSY.)

TOM: Bus shelters, doorways, alleyways . . . along the dock road
and down by the warehouses . . . Remember?

MARY: No.

JULIA: It sounds very romantic.

TOM: Until I got the car and then it was the back seat.

MARY: Tom . . .

TOM: We were insatiable!

MARY: You were!

TOM: Still am, love . . . still am!
(MARY *looks from* TOM *to* JULIA *and* SUSY, *embarrassed, a bit*

38

irritated. TOM *laughs and seizes her by the leg.* MARY *pushes his hand away.*)

She loves it really!

JULIA: All this conjugal affection has quite put me off my decorating.

MARY: Bye, Tom. Bye, Susy.

TOM: Bye.

(TOM *doesn't move.*)

JULIA: What are you doing with your week, Mary? Anything exciting?

MARY: If you can call Hoovering exciting.

JULIA: Hoovering?

MARY: Since I started work I've fallen way behind with the chores.

TOM: What week's this?

JULIA: Holiday rota.

TOM: When?

MARY: Two weeks from now.

TOM: You've got a week off? Great! We'll go to Majorca.

MARY: We'll what?

TOM: Majorca . . .

MARY: You're not off then.

TOM: I'll arrange it.

MARY: You can't arrange your holidays just like that.

TOM: I'll wangle it somehow.

MARY: Tom—all I'm planning—

TOM: Or tell you what . . . Susy, where was it you went with that party? You said it was knockout.

SUSY: Marrakesh.

TOM: That's it, we'll go there, Marrakesh.

MARY: I don't want to go to Marrakesh. Or to Majorca.

TOM: Where do you want to go?

MARY: I just want to stay here and catch up with the chores.

TOM: OK, we'll go the sandhills. To Freshfield. To the woods!

(TOM *laughs. Pecks* MARY *on the cheek. Winks at* JULIA. *Takes* SUSY *out.*)

MARY: I don't get it.

JULIA: What?

MARY: Tom . . .

JULIA: What about Tom?

MARY: You've seen him.

JULIA: I'm green with envy. (*Laughs.*) You should complain!

MARY: He's a bit overpowering.

JULIA: He's welcome to overpower me any night.

MARY: No . . . he's always been a good husband, I mean, steady, affectionate . . . but lately . . .

JULIA: What?

MARY: I don't know. Maybe it's me.

JULIA: Maybe it's you what?

MARY: Maybe I'm cold.

JULIA: You're never cold!

MARY: Well, not cold.

JULIA: You don't mean . . . frigid?

MARY: No. No, not frigid. That's all right. No, he's so high he leaves me feeling . . . sort of . . . oh, I don't know. (*Sips her drink.*) Like he wants to go to Marrakesh while I want to Hoover!

JULIA: I think you're just growing old!

MARY: So what's he growing? Young?

JULIA: Hmmm.

MARY: Look at this.

(MARY *shows an eternity ring she is wearing.*)

JULIA: I noticed it. Beautiful.

MARY: It should be. It cost a bomb. Tom insisted on buying it.

JULIA: He forced it on to your reluctant finger?

MARY: Yes. I wanted a new washing machine and he insists on buying an eternity ring!

JULIA: You're lucky.

MARY: I suppose I am.

JULIA: I can't see any man pressing an eternity ring on me.

MARY: You don't want one to.

JULIA: No . . . and yet, I have to admit that your husband is very fanciable.

MARY: Don't tell him . . . his head's big enough already!

JULIA: No, you are lucky.

MARY: So's he, isn't he?

JULIA: That's right, girl, don't underestimate yourself!

MARY: I won't.

(*Lights fade to blackout.*)

Lights up: Early evening in late September, almost three weeks later.
    SUSY *on the telephone.*

SUSY: How much? Fifteen? Fifteen a week? Fifteen a week each?
    It's a lot to find . . . I know it's the going rate. Yes, I know
    it's a nice area but it's still a lot to find. Me? No, I couldn't.
    You know why. It's just . . . Anyway my mum would have
    hysterics if she found out. She's not happy about the idea of
    me going into a flat at all . . . You know what she's like. I'll
    just have to sneak into independence! Independence phase
    one: a flat with the girls. (*Hears sounds from the hallway.*) I
    think that's them. Hey, they went to Freshfield for the day!
    Yes, to the sandhills! Crazy! It must have been freezing!
    Yes . . . Darby and Joan! Quite sweet really! All right, love.
    I'll be round.

(SUSY *puts down the telephone and begins collecting some study notes.*
    TOM *and* MARY *come in. They are well wrapped up and* TOM *carries
    a canvas bag containing a beach towel, newspaper, thermos flask,
    etc.*)

    What was it like?

TOM: Great.

SUSY: You went to the beach, did you?

TOM: Aye . . . and the woods.

SUSY: (*Laughs.*) Oh, aye.

TOM: Great out there. And we had it all to ourselves.

MARY: Not surprisingly.

TOM: Uh?

MARY: It was freezing.

TOM: It wasn't.

MARY: It was.

TOM: Warm enough in the woods, though, wasn't it?

(MARY *gives him a look.* TOM *winks at* SUSY. *Takes a cassette
    player and some tapes from the bag.* MARY *picks up the anorak
    which* TOM *has put on a chair. Goes to hang it in the hall.* TOM

selects a tape and plays it: 'Remember When', the Platters.
SUSY *is putting on her coat as* MARY *comes back.*)

MARY: I'm famished.

TOM: All that fresh air . . .

MARY: (*To* SUSY) You're going out?

SUSY: Yes.

MARY: Have you had your tea?

SUSY: I had a beefburger.

MARY: Why can't you make yourself a proper meal?

SUSY: I wasn't very hungry.

MARY: Where are you going? To see Nick?

SUSY: Yes.

MARY: Have you finished that essay?

SUSY: Nearly . . . I'm nearly there. It's going well.

MARY: Mmmm.

(SUSY *goes out.*)

She's seeing a lot of Nick, isn't she?

TOM: That's natural. He seems a nice lad.

MARY: She shouldn't let it interfere with her work.

TOM: Hey, Mary, remember that one?

(TOM *indicates the tape.*)

MARY: The teen ballads . . .

TOM: I think I'm enjoying a second adolescence.

MARY: You've grown very keen on your tapes.

TOM: Want me to turn it off?

MARY: No . . . well, d'you mind turning it down a bit?

(TOM *turns the tape down.*)

TOM: We should have taken our cozzies and had a swim.

MARY: The Mersey was poisonous enough twenty years ago—I wouldn't fancy it now.

(MARY *empties the canvas bag.*)

TOM: Didn't bother us then.

MARY: Nothing much did then.

TOM: What bothers you now?

MARY: Nothing.

TOM: Then what. . .?

MARY: Nothing. I didn't mean anything.

TOM: Remember how we always used to go back to your house

and have a salad tea?

MARY: Yes . . . swamped with salad cream.

TOM: And then we'd go to the dance.

MARY: Now we'll be watching TV.

TOM: You know . . . when you look at other married couples, people our own age . . . I think we're lucky, don't you?

MARY: In what way?

TOM: They slip into a routine.

MARY: You've got to have some routine.

TOM: I know, but . . .

MARY: What's so special about us? We get up, go to work, come home, watch TV and go to bed. Isn't that a routine?

(TOM *peers at* MARY'*s hair*.)

TOM: I see a silver thread among the gold there.

MARY: Look close, and you'll see a net of silver threads.

TOM: Well, routine or not . . . I still feel weak at the knees when I look at you. Like I did when I first saw you come walking into the dance hall. I'd feel just the same now!

MARY: You'd be lucky.

TOM: Eh?

MARY: That dance hall was shut down years ago. Now it's a supermarket.

TOM: You know what I mean.

MARY: Tom!

(MARY *looks at him, laughing*.)

TOM: What?

MARY: You've been listening to too many pop songs.

TOM: I mean it. I still feel like I did when you were 15.

(MARY *looks away from his urgency*.)

Do you?

MARY: Do I what?

TOM: D'you still feel like that?

MARY: Like what?

TOM: Like you did then.

MARY: What? Weak at the knees?

TOM: Yeah.

MARY: Oh . . . it's silly . . .

(MARY *goes into the kitchen with the bag and things*.)

43

TOM: What's silly about it?

(MARY *comes back in.*)

MARY: Fancy a pork chop?

TOM: What's silly about it?

MARY: Well . . . you can't feel the same after being married for twenty years . . . can you?

TOM: Why not?

MARY: Well . . .

TOM: I do. Only more.

MARY: Yes, but . . .

TOM: Don't you?

MARY: Yes, but it's got to be different.

TOM: Different?

MARY: Yes.

TOM: Why?

MARY: Oh, I don't know. This is silly.

(MARY *turns toward the kitchen.*)

TOM: Mary . . . wait. How is it different?

MARY: Well, you mature, don't you? Your feelings mature.

TOM: Mature?

MARY: Yes.

TOM: What d'you mean . . . mature?

MARY: I don't feel any less for you.

TOM: But different?

MARY: Yes.

TOM: How?

MARY: (*Sharp*) Why all these questions?

TOM: Look, Mary . . . with you and me . . . has it worked out the way you expected . . . the way you wanted?

MARY: Of course it has. We're married—we share a life. We're happy—we have a grown-up daughter. You've got a good job and I—I like mine. We're happy . . . what more . . .

TOM: Are *you* happy?

MARY: Oh, for God's sake!

(MARY *makes for the kitchen but* TOM *stands in front of her.*)

TOM: Sometimes I get the feeling that you're not happy at all. It's nothing I can put into words. Just something very faint . . . like the feeling of rain in the wind.

44

MARY: Do you talk like that on the docks?

　　(*They stare at each other.* MARY *turns away.*)

TOM: You're the only thing, Mary . . . the only thing . . . the only thing that matters to me. You know, don't you? You know that?

MARY: Yes.

TOM: You believe me?

MARY: Yes.

TOM: Mary . . .

MARY: (*Weary*) What?

TOM: This bloke Reece . . . Bob Reece . . .

MARY: What?

TOM: Do you . . . What do you think of him?

MARY: He's a drip. A nice drip.

　　(MARY *goes into the kitchen.* TOM *hesitates at the doorway. After a moment he follows her in. Blackout.*)

Loud music: 'River deep mountain high' by Ike and Tina Turner.

　　Lights up: The lounge, a little emptier now that Susy's bookcase has gone. It is some weeks later, about nine o'clock on an evening in October.

　　TOM, *wearing sweater and jeans, sits restlessly drinking from a can of beer. Checks his watch. Refills his glass.*

　　MARY *comes in from the hall, wearing office clothes.*

MARY: Hello, love.

　　(MARY *takes off her coat. Turns down the tape.*)

　　Oh, it's nice.

TOM: What?

MARY: (*Smiles.*) Being able to relax. Susy always seemed to want something!

TOM: Mmmm.

MARY: Did you sort out that problem with the union?

　　(TOM *shakes his head.* MARY *goes to him, kisses him.*)

TOM: Did you enjoy your drink?

MARY: Oh, I'm sorry I'm late again, love . . . but . . . Can you smell my breath?

TOM: Mmmm.

MARY: We just dropped in for a quickie . . . and well, you know Julia's quickies!

TOM: Julia's?

MARY: She wants to get a petition up about . . . this crackdown on spongers. She argues that more people are *not* claiming what they're entitled . . .

TOM: You and Julia?

MARY: Shall I make us something to eat?

TOM: No thanks.

MARY: Bacon and eggs? I'm famished.

TOM: No thanks. Did you have much to drink?

MARY: Oh, a few. Three or four. It's a bad habit. I must stop it.

TOM: You enjoy it, don't you?

MARY: It's nice to unwind . . .

TOM: Why stop it if you enjoy it?

(MARY *is about to go to the kitchen but stops and looks at* TOM.)

MARY: What happened with the union then?

TOM: They just refused to unload the cargo. Won't handle anything from Chile. No wonder the bosses fought so hard against unionization. But it's the Trots. One bloke in particular . . . there's always one . . . he could cause murder in an empty house.

MARY: But you can't be blamed . . . can you?

TOM: I'm to blame if anything goes wrong. That's what the boss thinks. I'm supposed to wave a magic wand and keep everybody working. Keep everything running smoothly. Only they haven't been running smoothly lately.

MARY: Well . . . you get these periods, don't you . . .

TOM: There was an accident on the dock today. Or . . . we're calling it an accident, anyway. Kershaw fell in the river.

MARY: Kershaw?

TOM: The docker I told you about. The one whose wife left him with the kids. Phil the pram. He drowned.

MARY: Oh, God . . .

TOM: They seem to think I should have sent him on sick leave. Maybe I should. He was drunk most of the time. But why couldn't he send himself on sick leave? A man must know whether he's sick or not.

MARY: Yes . . .

TOM: Anyway the boss had a go at me. (*Laughs.*) He asked me if

I'd got a fancy woman.

MARY: A what?

TOM: He seemed to think I was neglecting my job because I'd got a bit of skirt lined up somewhere.

MARY: What did you say?

TOM: I said I had.

(MARY *stares at* TOM.)

MARY: Would you . . . sure you wouldn't like an omelette or something?

TOM: No, thanks.

(MARY *moves toward the kitchen. Stops as* TOM *speaks*.)

But for the boss I would have picked you up at the office.

MARY: Oh, it's all right.

TOM: I mean, with him keeping me late, by the time I got to your office you'd gone.

MARY: Oh . . . you went round?

TOM: Yeah. What time did you go to the pub?

MARY: About half-five.

TOM: Crowd of you?

MARY: No . . .

TOM: What . . . just you and Julia?

MARY: Mmmm . . . I'm starving . . .

TOM: When did you leave?

MARY: About eight o'clock. The bus took ages. Fancy a coffee?

TOM: Why the hell do you have to lie?

MARY: What?

TOM: You were with Reece.

(MARY *is startled.* TOM *confronts her*.)

I saw you and Julia in the pub with Reece.

MARY: You saw us?

TOM: Yes, I saw you. I called at the office and the security man told me where you'd gone. So I looked in . . . and I saw you.

MARY: Why didn't you come and join us?

TOM: I didn't want to spoil the fun.

MARY: You should have come over . . .

TOM: Why didn't you say you were with Reece?

MARY: I wasn't 'with Reece'! I was with Julia . . . and Bob came in and joined us!

TOM: What's Julia then? The chaperone?

(MARY *turns away*.)

Why didn't you mention Reece?

MARY: Why do you think?

TOM: Eh?

MARY: Because I knew you'd throw a fit! Christ, you went down to the pub and spied on me and then came back here and waited . . . in order to trap me!

TOM: I'd say you trapped yourself.

MARY: And then you wonder why I didn't mention Bob!

TOM: Does he always go to the pub after work?

MARY: How would I know? I don't *always* go, do I?

TOM: Does he suggest you going?

MARY: Look Tom. Do you want me to stop going to the pub?

TOM: Do whatever you want to do.

MARY: If it bothers you that much, I'd rather not go. I mean, there's nothing in it, there's nothing to worry about . . . but if it really does bother you then I'd honestly prefer not to go.

TOM: You would?

MARY: Yes.

TOM: Honestly?

MARY: Yes.

TOM: You'd miss it, though . . .

MARY: (*Softer*) Tom . . . it doesn't matter . . . it isn't important to me . . .

TOM: I can't wait to get home to you.

MARY: I'll come straight home.

TOM: That's what gets me through the day.

MARY: I'm sorry, Tom . . . it was thoughtless of me . . . especially now Susy . . . The truth is, Bob and Julia have got into the habit of going to the pub once or twice a week after work . . . and I find it hard to say no. But really . . . it's silly . . .

TOM: I mean, if you like, we could always pop round to the local, couldn't we?

MARY: Yes . . .

TOM: It's a nice pub . . . friendly . . .

MARY: Yes . . .

TOM: But you never seemed keen on coming to the pub with me.

MARY: Well, I'm not really keen on pubs.

TOM: Oh. (*Studies* MARY.) So why do you go?

MARY: Well, like I said . . .

TOM: What?

MARY: I just find it hard to refuse . . .

TOM: To refuse the boss?

MARY: (*Wry*) I suppose that might be part of it.

TOM: And what's the other part?

MARY: What other part?

TOM: You like Reece, don't you?

MARY: He's all right.

TOM: Does he like you?

MARY: Yes, he's wild about me!

TOM: He does like you.

MARY: I don't know. Ask him.

TOM: I might. Do you fancy him?

MARY: Oh, for Christ's sake!

TOM: Mary, I'm sorry . . . I'm sorry . . . Wait . . .

MARY: You're forever grilling me!

TOM: I'm sorry . . . I didn't mean to . . . It's just . . . it's just that I was beginning to be afraid that you were happier with them than with me.

MARY: Them?

TOM: The office crowd . . . I was beginning to think that you were happier at work . . .

MARY: Oh Tom, honestly . . .

TOM: I thought maybe you looked at Julia and envied her her independence.

MARY: I don't envy Julia.

TOM: Honestly?

MARY: Honestly.

TOM: But she doesn't feel she has to rush home like you.

MARY: The only reason I might not want to rush home would be in case you were in a mood like tonight.

TOM: But she is free, isn't she? She's free to stay, or to leave,

49

whenever she feels like . . .

MARY: She gets the bus with me.

TOM: Does she?

MARY: Yes.

TOM: You bloody liar!

MARY: What?

TOM: Reece drove you back. He dropped Julia off and then he drove you back here. Not here, not to this house, but to the bus terminus! Why didn't he drive you home? Was that too close for comfort? Why didn't you say that Reece gave you a lift?

MARY: I said I'd get the bus but Bob insisted—

TOM: Oh, he insisted, did he?

MARY: How did you know all this?

TOM: Because I bloody well tailed you!

MARY: You tailed us!

TOM: I saw you park at the bus shelter. Ten minutes' walk from here, but it took you half an hour. Why so long? What were you doing? Why did it take you half an hour to get back from the shelter? I was waiting here for you . . .

(TOM *has seized* MARY'*s arms.*)

Were you walking very slow or what?

(MARY *frees herself.*)

MARY: I'm going to bed.

(MARY *goes to the stairs and up.* TOM *stands staring after her. Moves to follow. Stops. Stands, furious, desperate. Blackout.*)

Lights up: Next afternoon.

JULIA *sitting on the couch.*

After a moment MARY *comes downstairs. Both women are wearing their outdoor coats.* MARY *carries a towel and a toilet bag. She hurries to the sideboard and starts to look in the drawers.*

JULIA: Mary . . .

MARY: What?

JULIA: Don't you think you ought to have a talk with Tom?

MARY: What? After what he did this morning?

JULIA: Yes, but . . . well, what did he do? He asked Bob to leave you alone . . .

MARY: He didn't ask Bob to leave me alone. He told him to stop
pestering me. He stormed past the security guard into
Bob's office and shouted at him: 'Stop pestering my wife!'
(*Stuffs things into the bag.*) Julia, all I want to do is stay at
your place for a few days while I think things out . . .
decide what to do. I might be able to stay at Susy's for
a . . . God! How can I face Bob? (*Tearful*) And all the
others . . . It's all round the office!

JULIA: Oh, Bob will understand. He knows what Tom's like . . .
and as for the typing pool, well, they're absolutely
bubbling! Greatest day of their lives! The Civil Service has
never seen such drama before! You're a star, Mary, a star!
Enjoy it while you can. It'll be forgotten in nine days.

MARY: If anybody is pestering me, it isn't Bob—it's Tom. I
mean, waiting outside the office for me every night . . . all
right . . . but he rings me up five times a day as well! And
at the weekend . . . he even wants to come to the shops with
me! He wants to hold hands in the supermarket!

JULIA: Some women would love it.

MARY: Some women might. Not me. I'm . . . drained . . .

JULIA: Have you told him how you feel?

MARY: I can't. He wouldn't listen.

JULIA: He would if he knew he was driving you away. Talk to
him . . . see what he has to say.

MARY: There's nothing to say. There's nothing he could say that
would change my mind. I think he's ill.

JULIA: OK, so maybe he's suffering from stress . . . or the
menopause, or something. Maybe he should see a doctor?
(TOM *comes down the stairs. He's wearing sweater, jeans, slippers.
He stops and listens, unnoticed.*)

MARY: Or maybe I should. I don't know. I don't know what to
think. Sometimes I think it's my fault . . . I got so involved
with work I took him for granted.

JULIA: You couldn't have done any more. You've been a saint!

MARY: For over twenty years we had a marvellous relationship.
Tom was the most loving and loyal husband a woman
could dream of . . . I loved him dearly. I still do . . . but . . .

51

JULIA: But you need a break. Well, I'm tired of the telly, and the cat is no great conversationalist.

(TOM *comes down the stairs.*)

TOM: Hello there!

(JULIA *and* MARY *stare.*)

MARY: You're . . . home early . . .

TOM: I resigned.

MARY: You what?

TOM: I packed the job in.

MARY: You didn't!

TOM: Oh, I did.

MARY: Tom, if this is some sick joke . . .

TOM: No.

MARY: You resigned?

TOM: Yeah.

MARY: You mean you officially handed in notice?

TOM: (*Laughs.*) It wasn't exactly like that.

MARY: What then?

TOM: I told the boss to stuff the job up his arse.

MARY: Oh, Christ . . .

(MARY *looks in bewilderment at* JULIA.)

JULIA: What happened, Tom?

TOM: I put my coat on and walked out. Finito!

JULIA: But what led to it?

TOM: Nothing.

MARY: There must have been something, Tom.

TOM: I had a barney with the boss.

MARY: What about?

TOM: Nothing. He's an ould woman, always whingeing. He's been at me for months. All it was, there was a load of timber that had been lying on the dock for a few days, and he kept asking me to get it shifted. The lads said there was some problem with the dockets. So he started off again today . . . and I told him to stuff it.

MARY: Tom, you'll have to go in tomorrow and get this sorted out.

TOM: Get what sorted out?

MARY: You can't give up your job! You're crazy!

TOM: I'll find something.

MARY: What? Industry in this area is just crying out for men of 40, isn't it?

JULIA: Mary's right, Tom. We're dealing with men like that every day.

MARY: You'll have to go in and apologize.

TOM: Bugger that! I'm not making any apologies.

MARY: Well, you could smooth it over somehow, couldn't you?

TOM: I don't want to smooth it over.

MARY: Tom, if you don't go back to that job, you'll never get another one.

TOM: Fine.

MARY: But what'll you do?

TOM: I'll be the househusband.

MARY: Living on what?

TOM: On your lot, I suppose. And my pension . . . (*Touches* MARY's *chin*.) Chin up, love. Don't look so tragic!

MARY: But it is tragic, Tom! You were the best docks manager they ever had. You were proud of it, once. What happened?

TOM: Oh, it's all different now . . . with containerization and . . . I mean, the docks, the docks as I knew them . . . the docks are dying . . . the docker's a dying breed. You can't resist technical change, Mary. Can't live in the past! Eh, Julia? (JULIA *looks at him. Can't reply*.)

MARY: Tom . . .

TOM: What?

MARY: Before you throw your job away . . .

TOM: I have done.

MARY: Will you promise me one thing?

TOM: What?

MARY: Will you talk to the doctor?

TOM: The doctor?

MARY: Please . . .

TOM: What for?

MARY: For me.

TOM: Well . . . seems a bit . . . pointless . . .

MARY: I'll come with you.

TOM: Well, if . . . if it'll make you happier . . .

MARY: It will.

TOM: OK, but . . . you've got to understand, Mary . . . There's thousands of men round here without work now . . . my age, younger . . . older . . . like Julia said. It's no shame now, not working . . . it's no tragedy! I mean, I've worked all my life, but what do you work for? You don't work for work's sake, you work for your family, for the people you love. Now that Susy has flown the nest, there's only you and me, we've only got each other to think of, and I believe we could . . . The next years could be the best we've ever had! I'm really excited.

(TOM *looks from* MARY *to* JULIA. *He's aware of the bag on the floor.*)

Are you gonna take your coats off or shall I turn the heating up?

(MARY *hesitates. Then takes off her coat.*)

Let's all relax and have a drink!

(TOM *goes into the kitchen.* MARY *begins taking things from the bag and putting them back in the drawer. Lights fade to blackout.*)

Lights up: Two months later, a Saturday morning in December. Music: 'Stupid Cupid, Stop Picking on Me'.

TOM *comes from the hall wearing a bright shirt and jeans. Carries a Christmas tree. Puts it down and admires it. He gives a little shake to the music.*

MARY *looks from the kitchen doorway, as* TOM *does his dance.*

MARY: Isn't it a bit early for decorations?

TOM: Never too early! I'd have them up all the year round.

(MARY *shrugs, goes back to kitchen.* TOM, *in high spirits, dances back to the hall. Returns with a box containing lights and decorations. Takes these out. Begins threading the lights around the tree.* SUSY *comes in, wearing a heavy coat and carrying a bag.*)

SUSY: Hello, Dad!

TOM: Hello, love!

(TOM *hugs* SUSY.)

How's flat life? What are you after this time? Teaspoons, toilet paper? Towels? Or just a jar of marmalade?

SUSY: Tea towels. There's none . . .

TOM: Have you brought my prezzy?

SUSY: Not yet, Dad.

TOM: I wanna put it up on the tree. Hey, I've ordered a nice surprise for your mother. It won't go on the tree, though!

SUSY: What is it?

TOM: Ah, you'll have to wait.

SUSY: How've you been?

TOM: Fine. I've been fine. (*Leans close.*) Hey, you know she made me see a trick cyclist?

SUSY: What?

TOM: Your ma . . . made me see a psychologist. Young bird, it was. Scruggy. Arse hanging out of her jeans.

SUSY: Was she any help?

TOM: She gimme a lecture on sex and love. I thought she was gonna help me with the gas bill.

SUSY: Dad . . .

TOM: When I told her I was in love with my wife she looked at me as if I was daft. Seemed to think it was abnormal. Do you think it's abnormal?

SUSY: No, but . . .

TOM: Yes, young, she was a young bird, straight out of college. Full of textbook rubbish. She asked me if I'd ever loved anyone else. And when I said no, she said, 'Well, you loved your mother, didn't you?' 'Yes,' I told her, 'but I didn't sleep with my mother, did I?' Know what she replied? She said: 'I won't ask you if you wanted to!' Huh. She gimme these tapes.

(TOM *puts the tapes on the player.*)

Relaxation exercises, like . . . Listen . . .

(*The tape voice is very slow and measured.* TOM *mimics it.*)

CLOSE YOUR EYES . . . RAISE YOUR TONGUE TO . . . THE ROOF . . . OF YOUR MOUTH . . . (*Laughs.*) Yaaaa.

SUSY: Are they any good?

TOM: Yeah, can't you tell? I'm a new man now! Here, give us a hand with these deckies.

(TOM *gives* SUSY *some decorations to pin up.* SUSY *starts pinning.*)

How's Nick?

SUSY: He's working hard. You know he's decided to take—

TOM: Is he your lover?

SUSY: Dad . . .

(MARY *comes from the kitchen with a bag of laundry.*)

TOM: Have to keep an eye on her, Mary! She'll have the place stripped bare if we turn our backs! Hey, this is the first time in twenty-one years she'll be out of the way at Chrimbo! We'll have a party! I bet she's back for her presents and her Christmas dinner, though!

SUSY: You bet.

(MARY *goes back to the kitchen.*)

Dad . . . are you going to the match today?

TOM: Er . . . no.

SUSY: Nick has been asking everywhere for a ticket. They're like gold.

TOM: Might be able to get one at the ground if he's willing to pay over the odds. I wouldn't do it, though.

SUSY: I wondered if you'd mind lending him your season ticket.

(MARY *returns with a second bag of laundry.*)

TOM: Yeah, sure.

MARY: It's the Derby game, isn't it?

TOM: Yes.

MARY: And you're not going?

TOM: I want to get these decorations finished.

SUSY: Thanks, Dad. It's bound to be a full house.

MARY: What's the point of having a season ticket if you're going to pick and choose your matches?

SUSY: At least it means you can always get in to the big games.

MARY: Yes, but he's not going to the big game, is he? And they're not cheap, those season tickets.

(*A knock at the door.* SUSY *goes. Comes back, looking puzzled.*)

Who is it?

SUSY: It's a man from the garage.

MARY: The garage?

SUSY: He's brought a new car. A white sports car. It's in the road now.

MARY: A sports car?

SUSY: (*Near laughter*) Yes, outside. He says Dad ordered it.

(MARY *looks at* TOM, *who concentrates on the tree. She goes out.* *Sound of raised voices from outside.* MARY *comes back.*)

MARY: (*To* TOM) Did you order that car?

TOM: No.

(MARY *is holding a form from the garage. She looks at this.*)

MARY: God, I'd better ring the garage.

SUSY: Mum . . . have you got a spare pair of tights?

MARY: In the bedroom. Second drawer.

(SUSY *goes upstairs.* MARY *lifts the phone. Listens. Dials. Listens again.*)

What's wrong with the phone?

(TOM *keeps busy.*)

It's dead. Tom, the phone is dead. You paid the bill, didn't you?

TOM: I'm not sure . . .

MARY: Oh Christ, Tom! We had a threat to disconnect two weeks ago . . . where is it? I told you to pay.

TOM: I forgot all about it.

(MARY *looks in a drawer. Finds a large envelope and takes out some bills.*)

MARY: Yes, seven days' notice to pay. Oh, you're hopeless, Tom! What are these? What's this? The mortgage?

TOM: Don't worry . . .

MARY: Have you paid the mortgage?

TOM: I'll deal with it.

MARY: You haven't paid the mortgage?

TOM: I was gonna write to them.

MARY: We'll lose the bloody house!

TOM: We'll manage . . . somehow . . .

MARY: How will we manage?

TOM: They'll give us time to pay.

MARY: Yes, and what then? How will we pay then?

TOM: No panic . . . I could . . . er, I could sell the car.

MARY: You haven't even finished paying for that yet. You're crazy. You haven't even registered as unemployed, have you? You could have been drawing the dole, at least.

TOM: I don't want it.

MARY: You don't want it? Too proud, are you? Won't stoop to

57

charity? You're the Government's dream, you are!

TOM: I'll pay the bills.

MARY: You mean *I'll* pay the bills.

TOM: No.

MARY: So how will you pay?

TOM: We could have lodgers.

MARY: Lodgers?

(SUSY *comes downstairs with the packet of tights.*)

You found them all right.

SUSY: Yes. And these.

(SUSY *has a cheeky grin. Shows an envelope. Takes out the Polaroid snaps that* TOM *and* MARY *had taken.*)

MARY: What?

SUSY: You make a lovely couple!

MARY: Give me those!

(MARY *takes the snaps and puts them back in the envelope.*)

SUSY: You could sell those to one of those magazines. Or are you keeping them for the album?

(MARY *gives* SUSY *a look. Starts lugging the laundry bag to the hall.*)

TOM: Hang on.

MARY: What?

TOM: Let me do that.

(TOM *carries the bags to the hall.* MARY *puts her coat on.* TOM *gets his coat.*)

MARY: I'm going to the laundrette.

TOM: (*Smiles.*) I didn't think you were going to church, love. I'll carry the bags for you. They're a weight.

MARY: Don't bother, I can manage.

TOM: It's all right. I'll come up with you.

MARY: There's no point in both of us going.

TOM: I don't mind.

(SUSY *has been fiddling with the lights on the tree. Now turns them on.*)

SUSY: (*A fanfare*) DADADA! Christmas!

TOM: Lovely!

SUSY: God, I used to look forward to that when I was little.

TOM: So did I. When you were little.

58

(SUSY *resumes sticking up decorations.*)

MARY: Tom, if you really want to help with the laundry . . .

TOM: Aye.

MARY: Then you take it up and do it.

TOM: Eh?

MARY: I've got lots of other things I could do. Here . . .

(MARY *gets a box of soap powder from the kitchen. Puts it on a table. Then puts down cash.*)

You'll need a fifty pence piece for each washing machine . . . one bag to each. Twenty pence for the extractor . . . and some more twenties for the drier. There's towels in there, so give them at least four dries . . . two quid. God, it's so expensive! We should have got a new washing machine years ago, it would have paid for itself by now. But you would buy that ring . . .

(TOM *looks at the money for a moment. Puts the laundry bags down.*)

TOM: It would solve all our problems, you know.

MARY: What would?

TOM: What I said . . .

MARY: Lodgers?

TOM: Yeah.

MARY: Turn the place into a boarding house! I don't want lodgers, Tom, thank you.

TOM: One would do.

MARY: One?

TOM: Yeah.

MARY: Oh . . . and do you have anyone in mind?

TOM: Yeah.

MARY: Who?

TOM: I've already made enquiries.

MARY: Who?

TOM: I talked it over with your mates last night.

MARY: Who?

TOM: Julia and Bob Reece.

MARY: You talked it over with them? Where?

TOM: In the pub last night.

MARY: What . . . you went to the pub where . . .

TOM: Yeah, after work. I was thinking, it might be a good idea to rent a room, but you've got to be careful about who you take on, haven't you? And I suddenly thought, what about Bob Reece? I mean, he seems a reliable sort of feller, Bob Reece.

MARY: Bob Reece . . .

TOM: Aye . . . make a good lodger . . .

MARY: You went and talked to Bob . . .

TOM: Aye. I put it to him, like . . .

MARY: You did what?

TOM: I offered him a room with us. Low rent. He'd have his own room . . . share bathroom and kitchen. Perfect. I told him he'd be very welcome, from my point of view. And I said, *you* would be over the moon. It'd suit everyone, it's an ideal arrangement, couldn't be better. Rent monthly in advance, of course. No deposit, I think we could skip the deposit with Bob Reece, don't you? Anyway . . . he didn't give me a definite answer. He seemed a bit . . . taken aback . . . surprised, like. Couldn't believe his luck. I think he wants to think it over for a bit.

(MARY *looks at* TOM *with disbelief for a moment. Then with contempt.*)

MARY: You vicious bastard.

(MARY *goes out.* TOM *stands looking after her. Turns to* SUSY.)

TOM: D'you see that? D'you hear that? What's the matter with her? Ever since she got that job your mother's been . . . It's her should be on the doctor, not me!

(SUSY *comes over to* TOM. *Touches his arm.*)

SUSY: Take it easy, Dad.

(SUSY *goes to the hall.*)

TOM: (*Panicky*) Susy, what are you . . . where are you . . . You're not going?

SUSY: Only to the laundrette. I'll be back.

TOM: I'll come with you. Can I come with you?

(*They collect the things and go out. Lights fade to blackout.*)

Music: 'You've lost that loving feeling' by the Righteous Brothers.
   Lights up on tree: The room is dimly lit by the fairy lights on the tree,

60

revealing TOM *sitting absolutely still. Later the same day, about nine o'clock.*

  Music stops. TOM *starts whistling a strange, discordant parody of the song, hardly recognizable. Door bangs.* TOM *stops whistling.* MARY *comes in. Puts on the light. Looks at* TOM, *who stares straight ahead. After a moment* MARY *goes upstairs.* TOM *gives a brief glance at the stairs.* MARY *comes down with the bag. Goes to the drawer, stuffs some things in the bag, as before.* MARY *closes the zip and stands.*

MARY: Tom.

  (TOM *doesn't respond.*)

  Tom, I'm going to stay with Julia for a while.

  (*Still no response.*)

  I think it's the best thing . . . (*Picks up the bag. Turns away.*)
  All right? I'll ring you next week.

  (*Goes toward the hall. Stops. Turns to look at* TOM, *who still sits staring ahead.*)

  We'll have to talk, Tom.

  (TOM *suddenly turns and looks at her.*)

  I'd hoped . . . I'd hoped that these last couple of months
  would be different . . . that you'd find a job, any sort of job,
  and . . . adjust . . . and we'd be happy again, like we used
  to be. But it's no good, Tom, we're just getting at each
  other . . . just torturing each other. I haven't been
  happy . . . and I know you haven't. So . . . And then the
  mortgage and all the other bills . . . I mean, we're just
  sinking! So . . . I thought, if I stay with Julia for a while . . .
  and maybe you could stay with Susy at her place . . . We've
  got to have time to think, to see where we're going. Maybe
  we could sell the house. Find a small flat. Start again. We
  could help each other . . .

TOM: Been with Bob?

MARY: Yes.

TOM: I knew it! How is lover boy, by the way? (*Stands.*) He is
  your lover, isn't he? Go on, you can tell me now, doesn't
  matter now, you might as well tell me. I won't hit you. He
  is your lover, isn't he?

MARY: No.

TOM: No?

(TOM *goes to* MARY.)

No? What's wrong with him then? He knew you liked him.
You did like him, didn't you?

MARY: Yes, I liked him.

TOM: I knew you did!

MARY: He's a good man.

TOM: Oh aye!

MARY: I like him because he's gentle, and he has a generous
spirit.

TOM: Oh aye? Bloody poofter, is he? Bumboy? One of them?

(MARY *picks up the bag.* TOM *takes hold of it too.*)

Is that what was wrong?

MARY: No.

(MARY *tries to pull the bag away.* TOM *pulls it back.*)

TOM: So what was wrong? Huh . . . didn't he fancy you after all?

(MARY *tugs at the bag again but* TOM *holds on to it.*)

MARY: He asked me to marry him.

TOM: Marry him!

MARY: Yes.

TOM: What . . . a formal proposal?

MARY: Yes.

TOM: Yeah, well . . . remember . . . you're still married to me.
You're still my wife.

(TOM *pulls the bag away from* MARY *and tosses it behind him.*)

What did you say?

MARY: I said no.

TOM: Why?

MARY: I don't want to marry him.

TOM: Oh, you don't?

MARY: No, I don't.

TOM: You like him, though. You said you liked him. He is your
lover, isn't he?

MARY: He tried.

TOM: Tried? What do you mean, he tried?

(TOM *grabs* MARY's *wrists.*)

What do you mean he tried?

MARY: (*Struggling*) You know what I mean.

TOM: No I don't no I don't!

62

(MARY *gets free and walks past* TOM *to the bag. Picks it up.* TOM
bars the way.)
What happened? You had a necking session, I suppose? At
the flat? Or earlier, before that? You had a necking session?
In the office? Or in the car? In the back of the car? You
went for a few drinks and a drive and then you had a
necking session in the back of the car? You like the back of
the car, don't you?

MARY: Yes.

TOM: You had a necking session?

MARY: Yes.

TOM: And he touched you up, I suppose?

MARY: Yes.

TOM: He touched you on the breasts?

MARY: Yes.

TOM: On the dress . . . or under . . . on the bra . . . or . . . or
under, on the breasts . . .

MARY: On the breasts.

TOM: On the skin?

MARY: On the skin.

TOM: On the skin!

MARY: Yes.

TOM: On the skin where. . . ? Where? Where exactly? On the
skin . . . on the nipple?

MARY: On the nipple.

TOM: On the nipple!

MARY: Yes.

TOM: And you didn't stop him, you didn't object, you didn't
mind, you were enjoying it . . .

MARY: Yes.

TOM: And he said he loved you . . .

MARY: Yes.

TOM: And what did you say, you said I love you too . . .

MARY: Yes.

TOM: And he kissed you, he kissed you with the tongue . . .

MARY: Yes.

TOM: And then he stroked you, he stroked you and felt your
legs . . .

63

MARY: Yes.

TOM: And then he pulled your tights down . . .

MARY: No.

TOM: Eh?

MARY: No. I did that.

TOM: What? What went wrong then? Isn't he up to it? What's wrong with him? Is he impotent or something? Couldn't he satisfy you?

MARY: He satisfied me.

TOM: Oh, did he?

MARY: Yes. Completely.

(TOM *slaps* MARY *viciously. She falls back, dropping the bag.* TOM *stares at her, shocked.* MARY *scrambles up.* TOM *hurries to help her but she rejects his help.*)

TOM: Oh Christ, Mary, I'm sorry . . . Mary . . . I didn't mean . . . I'd never hurt you . . .

(MARY *picks up the bag and goes.*)

Mary . . . Mary . . .

(*But she has gone.* TOM *turns back, moaning. Sees the Madonna statuette. Seizes it and smashes it against the table. Falls to his knees with the fragments, moaning.*)

(*Blackout.*)

ACT TWO

The scene is Mary's flat over a pub. A spacious elegant room with a high ceiling, recently deocrated, but looking a little bare. Left, door to hall (off). Two other doors, to kitchen and bathroom (off). Stripped wooden floor with an Indian carpet. Sparsely furnished with a couch, scattered cushions, music centre. Standard lamp.

It is a hot evening in August, eight months later. Intermittent noises from the pub below and bursts of reggae music.

MARY *is fiddling with the plug for the standard lamp.* JULIA *is lugging the couch around.* SUSY *comes in from kitchen with a tray carrying a bottle of plonk and three glasses. All are wearing old casual gear.* SUSY *pours three glasses. Looks at* MARY.

SUSY: (*Smiles.*) How are you getting on?

MARY: I see I'll have to brush up on the electrics.

SUSY: Here, let's see.

(SUSY *takes the plug and begins fixing it.*)

JULIA: Give us a hand with this, Mary.

(MARY *helps* JULIA *to move the couch. They scrutinize it critically.*)

Doesn't look right there, does it?

MARY: Let's try it over there.

(*They move the couch around.*)

SUSY: Is this the only electric point?

MARY: Yes.

SUSY: That's always the problem with these old flats, isn't it?

JULIA: Mine's just the same. You'll have to get an extension lead and an adaptor.

MARY: A what?

JULIA: (*Laughs.*) Never mind for now.

(SUSY *lights the lamp.*)

SUSY: DADA!

MARY: Brilliant! She's a technical genius!

SUSY: Mum, fixing a plug doesn't make you a technical genius.

MARY: It does in my book. Anyway, you fixed the washer as well.

SUSY: Oh, it's Dad. Since he's been in the flat I've had a crash course in home maintenance.

JULIA: I knew Tom would be handy like that.

SUSY: In six months he's transformed the place. The plumbing, the electrics . . . the landlord is laughing!

(*They take a drink.*)

JULIA: How does he get on with the students?

SUSY: Well, he's not the easiest person to live with.

JULIA: Why?

SUSY: He's not the ideal communard. He can't understand why everything is so disorganized.

JULIA: And why is it?

SUSY: That's the way we like it! All arrangements are provisional! You know, you make an arrangement with the understanding that either of you may or may not keep it. We like to be spontaneous. (*Laughs.*) Dad said it takes a lot of careful planning to be spontaneous!

JULIA: He's right about that.

SUSY: He's very fair. He stocks up the fridge . . . and then he's amazed when he returns and finds it empty.

MARY: But he warned *you* about that, didn't he?

SUSY: Well, he's forgotten his own lesson. He's always going on about his tea and his sugar and . . . you know, *his* tea and *his* sugar!

MARY: I don't know if I'd be good at sharing with a crowd.

JULIA: He's not very popular, then?

SUSY: Oh, it's not that bad. They just think, oh . . . different generation. Though one of the girls quite fancies him.

MARY: Who's that?

SUSY: Girl called Linda. Mind you, she fancies anything in trousers.

MARY: Has he said anything about getting his own place?

SUSY: No.

MARY: Well . . . now that he's got the money from the house . . .

SUSY: Yes . . . I've told him I'm going next month . . . so . . .

JULIA: Where are you going?

MARY: She's moving in with Nick.

JULIA: Really?

MARY: She's virtually been living with Nick for the last year.

JULIA: Have you?

SUSY: Yes, so we thought it would be simpler to—

JULIA: Share the rent?

SUSY: Exactly.

MARY: Did your father ever say anything. . . ?

SUSY: No. He accepts that . . . well, that's how people are now.

MARY: How are they nowadays?

SUSY: Oh, you know . . . half the students live with someone . . .
for a while, anyway . . . They try it. And if it doesn't
work . . . (*Shrugs.*) Dad's quite liberal about all that.

MARY: Oh, he can be very liberal when he doesn't care.

JULIA: I think people have a much healthier attitude to sex these
days. To sex before marriage, anyway.

SUSY: It's not just before marriage, Julia.

JULIA: Hm?

SUSY: Half the married students are having affairs.

JULIA: Adultery!

SUSY: Call it that . . . it's nothing.

MARY: Nothing?

SUSY: (*Defiant*) No.

MARY: Adultery's nothing, and fidelity's everything.

SUSY: What?

MARY: I can't believe it's all really as casual . . . as painless . . .
as you're making out.

SUSY: I didn't say it was painless.

JULIA: But then it wasn't painless when people made such a big
deal out of fidelity.

MARY: What about Nick?

SUSY: What?

MARY: Would you care if he was unfaithful?

SUSY: I don't feel easy with the word . . . but, well . . . I might
care but I wouldn't make an issue out of it. I mean . . . I
didn't make an issue out of it.

MARY: Oh, I see. I'm sorry. I really wasn't trying to probe.

SUSY: It's all right. After all, he didn't make an issue out of it
when I . . .

MARY: You?

SUSY: Yes.

MARY: And Nick knew you were . . . unfaithful?

SUSY: I have never been unfaithful to Nick. I may have been seduced, but never unfaithful.

(SUSY *and* JULIA *laugh,* MARY *looks wry.*)

JULIA: So what are you planning?

SUSY: One more year here, in Liverpool, and then America. We hope. We've written to a number of universities . . .

JULIA: And . . . marriage?

SUSY: Hopefully not. (*Refills the glasses.*) Here's to liberation!

JULIA: Cheers.

MARY: I hope you don't see me as a symbol of liberation, Susy.

SUSY: But you are.

MARY: Don't count on it.

SUSY: You said that the last six months, living with Julia, had been the best six months of your life.

MARY: They have.

SUSY: Well, if you've enjoyed yourself so much . . .

MARY: I have. But not on principle. I just made the best of things.

SUSY: I think . . . oh, it doesn't matter.

MARY: No, what? Go on.

SUSY: Lots of the students come from . . . what they used to call 'broken homes'.

JULIA: They still do.

SUSY: Yeah, but, I mean, it's no big deal now. It's almost the norm. I think you . . . and Julia . . . your generation . . . were precursors.

JULIA: Precursors of what, though?

SUSY: Some new kind of relationship. Your generation was the first one where marriage breakdown became common. Or commonplace. Your generation married for love. And then split for love. Love was the reason . . . or the excuse.

JULIA: I still don't know what we are precursors of.

SUSY: Well, if your generation outgrew marriage, I think my generation have outgrown love.

MARY: Oh really?

SUSY: Yes, I mean love as some sort of religious mania, where the two people devote themselves to each other and forget the whole world. That's just crazy.

68

MARY: It may be crazy but it's real.

JULIA: But Mary, Susy has a point.

SUSY: The fact that it's real doesn't mean that it's natural. If anything *is* natural. After all, why are we drinking this wine? Because in our society people drink wine. In other societies they wouldn't. Why do we eat meat? Because in our society people eat meat. Why do men wear trousers? Because—

MARY: So you think that love is just conforming with what society expects?

SUSY: Do you ever listen to the lyrics of pop songs? They're about nothing else!

JULIA: It isn't just pop songs, Susy.

SUSY: What?

JULIA: Romeo and Juliet? Dante and Beatrice? Tristan and Isolde? Queen Victoria mourning Albert for the rest of her life in glorious widowhood? Forget the pop songs . . . Love dominates the poetry and the novels and the plays and the operas . . . Is it surprising that we want a part, even a little part, a walk-on, in the universal drama?

MARY: Everything you say may be true and yet . . .

JULIA: (*Smiles.*) And yet what?

MARY: You can only go by your own experience.

JULIA: So?

MARY: Well, I don't know . . . maybe love is 'the sweetest thing'!

JULIA: And the sourest . . .

MARY: That's true too.

JULIA: Love is just an excuse for sexual harassment.

SUSY: Mum, would you contemplate ever getting married again?

MARY: Oh, I . . . I don't know. I'd have to get divorced first!

SUSY: Don't evade the question.

MARY: I pass.

JULIA: I think friendship is a much nobler emotion.

SUSY: Yes. It's not so parasitic.

JULIA: Why couldn't you stay with me? I shall be desolate now!

MARY: For the first time in my life I've got my own place. You know, in my whole life, I've never had my own place before. Nobody to answer to when I come back. And my

own job. And my own friends . . . and I've even got my
own money in the bank too! What more do I need?
(*They laugh, drink.*)

SUSY: I think Julia is right.

MARY: How?

SUSY: I think the love of the future will be a kind of charged
friendship.

MARY: Who pays the charge?
(*A knock at the door.* MARY *goes to open it. Comes back with* TOM.
His lip is bloody. He is wearing a scruffy sweater and jeans.)

TOM: Mind if I come in?

MARY: What's happened to you?

TOM: Oh, some kids . . .
(SUSY *and* JULIA *jump up.*)

SUSY: Kids?

TOM: A bunch of kids walking in a line on the pavement as if
they owned it. I should have stepped off.
(SUSY *goes off to the bathroom.*)
Got yourself a nice place, Mary.

MARY: Mmmm.

TOM: Over a pub! Perfect! How did you find it?

JULIA: It's my local . . . I know the landlord.

TOM: Perfect!
(SUSY *comes back with a wet flannel.*)

SUSY: Here.

TOM: It's OK.
(SUSY *wipes the cut.*)
Linda told me you were here. Thought I'd just . . . drop
in . . .
(SUSY *gives* TOM *the cloth.*)

SUSY: You'd better hold that, Dad.

TOM: Ta. Just moved in, eh?

MARY: Yes.

SUSY: Like a drink?

TOM: Ta.
(SUSY *goes off to the kitchen.*)
Yeah, it's a nice place, this. Bound to be a bit noisy, of
course.

70

MARY: I like that.

TOM: Yeah . . . lively.

(TOM *dabs his face. Looks at* JULIA. *She goes off after* SUSY.)
You rent it, eh?

MARY: Yes.

TOM: Have to find a place myself soon.

MARY: You ought to . . .

TOM: Haven't got a room upstairs, have you? (*Laughs. Walks around the room.*) I'd like that, living over a pub.

MARY: There aren't any other flats here, Tom.

TOM: Oh? Pity, that . . . Mind you, the area is a shithouse.

(SUSY *comes from the kitchen and gives* TOM *a can of beer and a glass.*)
Ta, love.

(SUSY *looks at him. Returns to the kitchen.* MARY *follows him with her eyes as he wanders around the room.*)
I always fancied living central. Living in town. It was you wanted to go and live in the suburbs.

MARY: I did then.

TOM: Bit of a change, isn't it? From a suburban cemetery to the heart of the bloody riot area? Red light area? Think you'll like it?

MARY: Tom, I've lived with Julia for six months and more . . .

TOM: Oh aye. You moved fast enough.

MARY: What?

TOM: Once the money came through.

MARY: I didn't want to impose on Julia.

TOM: I thought she wanted you there.

(MARY *looks at* TOM.)

MARY: Why have you come, Tom?

TOM: Just to see you were all right.

MARY: I'm not your responsibility any more.

TOM: I like your music centre.

(TOM *examines the tapes.*)

MARY: I'm not coming back, Tom.

TOM: Hey, half of these tapes are mine!

(TOM *plays a tape: 'When I'm 64', the Beatles.*)

MARY: Tom, what are you going to do?

71

TOM: About what?

MARY: Well, Susy's moving in with Nick . . . and you can't be happy staying in a student flat . . .

TOM: What . . . with all those nubile young women?

MARY: Tom . . .

TOM: I'm having the time of my life.

MARY: Tom, for the first time in your life, you've got some money. You've got twelve thousand pounds in the bank and the chance to . . . What are you going to do?

TOM: That house with the bronze numberplate three doors down . . . you know it's a knocking shop? Jumping all day and night. I've had some fun in there! Haven't you got any chairs?

MARY: What are you going to do with the money?

TOM: This last year, I've had the time of my life! I tell you, the way things are going, they'll do it for a bar of chocolate! In the old days, when I looked at a woman, I had to undress her. Now I have to dress her! There's no mystery any more. A naked woman means nothing to me. Unless she's properly wrapped, I can't even get a hard-on.

(MARY *turns away. Takes her wine. Sits.*)

That shock you, eh?

(MARY *ignores him.*)

Women, they're threepence off, these days!

MARY: What . . . are you going to do with the money?

TOM: I don't know, I might just fuck myself to death.

MARY: You'll have to leave Susy's.

TOM: I know.

MARY: Why don't you buy a place?

TOM: I don't wanna buy a place, I'm a gypsy, a nomad. How's Reece?

(MARY *stands and goes toward the kitchen.* TOM *bars the way.*)

I'm thinking of buying a cab.

MARY: A cab?

TOM: Yeah . . . think it's a good idea?

MARY: If you do . . .

TOM: There's bags of variety. Might suit me. What do you think?

MARY: Yes . . . I think it's a good idea.

TOM: See the world . . .

MARY: Yes.

TOM: I'll give you the number. Radio cab, of course.

MARY: Yes.

TOM: Sit down for a minute.

(MARY *sits.* TOM *stands.*)

I've learned a lot this last year.

MARY: Oh?

TOM: Yeah . . . I go down the Pier Head, have a cup of tea, look at the river. Think of all the ships that once sailed down that river. All the sailors, over the centuries. Some of them didn't come back, of course. One of my uncles sailed away and never came back. What happened to him? It was always a mystery in the family. In the old days, when things got too tough, you could always go down to the docks and jump a banana boat to Cuba. Imagine it! Escape! I'm 41.

MARY: I know.

TOM: What do we want?

MARY: What . . . you?

TOM: It all just flows away, doesn't it?

MARY: What?

TOM: Think of all the people who've drowned in that river. Kershaw. Poor old Phil the Pram. They fished him out. Now he's six feet deep. Why? What for? You can keep the money.

MARY: What money?

TOM: What use is twelve thousand pounds to me?

MARY: It's yours, Tom . . . it's your share.

TOM: My share?

MARY: Yes.

TOM: Is that what our life added up to? Twice twelve? Twenty-four grand?

MARY: Tom, that's just the house . . .

TOM: Who's there now? Who's living in it now? Who sleeps in the room we slept in? Strangers have taken over! I walked past it, you know. More than once. They've got a big hedge around the garden, you can't see in. I wanted to knock on the door and ask for a look around but they would've thought I was daft, wouldn't they? You can't live in the past, can you?

MARY: No.

TOM: You seem to be all right, then.

MARY: Yes.

TOM: No hard feelings?

MARY: No.

TOM: Forgiven me, have you?

MARY: There's nothing to forgive.

TOM: And you don't feel . . . anything . . .

MARY: No.

TOM: Good. Good. Clean slate. Well, I mean, at 41 . . . it's only half-time, isn't it, there's a lot could happen before the final whistle! You're born, you grow old, you die . . . you've got to make the most of each phase, haven't you?

MARY: That's what I'm trying to do.

TOM: Yes. Of course. I don't suppose you can imagine young women finding me attractive, can you?

MARY: What?

TOM: Ask Susy. Go on, ask her.

MARY: Tom, I never thought you were not attractive.

TOM: Oh, you still find me attractive?

MARY: Tom, stop. Please stop.

TOM: I've never had any trouble getting women, you know.

MARY: Please stop!

TOM: Even when we were together I had plenty of women.

MARY: I'm sure you were a real Casanova.

TOM: You don't believe me?

MARY: I believe you had women in your mind.

TOM: My mind? My mind was swimming in women. I never stopped thinking about women. Even when we were making love I was thinking of other women. Don't try and tell me about women. I know about women.

MARY: Tom, I hope you do get to know some other women. I really do. I hope you stop fantasizing and get to know some flesh-and-blood women.

TOM: (Calls) Susy!

74

(SUSY *comes in.* JULIA *stands behind her.*)

SUSY: What?

TOM: Your mother seems to think I'm past it.

SUSY: Past. . . ?

TOM: Tell her what Linda said.

MARY: Don't bother.

TOM: Go on, tell her. Tell her what your mate Linda said about
me.

SUSY: She said she found you attractive.

TOM: That's not what you told me! What did she say exactly?

SUSY: Well . . .

TOM: Go on!

SUSY: She said you made her feel sexy.

(TOM *turns triumphantly to* MARY. MARY *looks at him. Goes to
kitchen.*)

Mum . . . I . . .

(SUSY *follows* MARY.)

JULIA: Tom, what the hell are you doing?

TOM: Just getting a few things straight.

JULIA: Are you trying to kill any feeling Mary has for you?

TOM: Oh, she still has some feeling for me, does she? That's nice,
I'm grateful for that.

JULIA: The only thing that surprises me is that she put up with
you for so long.

TOM: Oh, it was all my fault, was it?

JULIA: Yes, it was. You treated her as if you owned her.

TOM: It was mutual, wasn't it?

JULIA: What?

TOM: One flesh.

JULIA: What do you mean?

TOM: We were married. We got married in church. We took the
vows.

JULIA: Oh, you owned her and she owned you.

TOM: I didn't want us to separate. I never wanted a life separate
from Mary. I don't want one now. I know you won't
believe me . . . but without Mary I don't really want to live.

JULIA: That's absurd.

TOM: Is it?

75

JULIA: What if she died?

TOM: That'd be easier.

JULIA: What you mean is . . . you can't stand Mary having a life separate from you.

TOM: Yes.

JULIA: Even if that's what *she* wants.

TOM: Yes.

JULIA: What you feel isn't love.

TOM: Whatever it is, I can tell you this . . . I often wish I didn't feel it. I wish I felt nothing for her. I wish I didn't know of her existence. I wish that I'd never met her!

JULIA: You don't feel love . . . you're too selfish to love.

TOM: Is it selfish for me to want my wife to love me?

JULIA: It's selfish to demand it regardless of what she wants.

TOM: I am talking about my wife.

JULIA: You're talking about your slave, not your wife. You can't chain your partner to you forever.

TOM: Yeah, well . . . I thought marriage was forever.

JULIA: No longer, Tom. These days you've got to be tolerant.

TOM: Tolerant?

JULIA: You've got to have some humility toward your partner. You've got to recognize their needs.

TOM: Needs?

JULIA: Mary is right. Your problem is you know nothing about women. You believe you were lucky that you met Mary when you were very young and fell in love and got married, don't you?

TOM: Huh . . . I used to . . .

JULIA: That was the worst thing that could have happened for both of you.

TOM: Why?

JULIA: You fell in love with the first woman you ever slept with. Can I say something very personal? I doubt if you have ever slept with anyone else. Have you?

TOM: What does that matter?

JULIA: Have you?

TOM: As it happens . . . no. Should I be ashamed?

JULIA: You must have wanted to, though.

76

TOM: OK, I have fancied the odd bird. But that's normal, isn't it? Normal weakness.

JULIA: Why do you call it a weakness?

TOM: What . . . you think I would have been better if I'd been jumping in and out of bed with all sorts of partners when I was in my teens?

JULIA: I think everyone would be.

TOM: You don't think I was right to wait?

JULIA: Wait for what?

TOM: You don't think people should wait until they're emotionally ready for sex?

JULIA: If everybody had to wait until they were emotionally ready for sex, most people would never make it. They'd be virgins all their life.

TOM: You know, I'm beginning to understand what happened to Mary.

JULIA: What?

TOM: You talk about love when all you can see and hear and think about is sex. You talk about not chaining anyone when the truth is you can't hold a man for five minutes. I think you were jealous of what Mary and I had. You wanted it to fail! What do you know about love? Who are you to preach? Respect Mary's needs, you say. Don't I have needs? You know who you sound like? You sound like that bloody psychologist I saw. Got all the answers pat. She went on about sleeping with people . . . asked me if I ever wanted to sleep with my mother! You go on about humility, my daughter . . . my own daughter . . . lectures me about freedom! Even the priest . . . the priest! . . . gave me a sermon about compassion and tolerance! What about commitment? Doesn't anybody believe in commitment any more? I would have given up the world for Mary! Don't any of you understand? I loved her. I still love her. Are you all hypocrites or am I crazy? You all think I'm crazy, don't you? You, and Susy, and . . . and even Mary herself! You think I'm crazy because I love my wife. My wife! (*Sits on the couch, burying his head.*) Get away from me. (JULIA *goes to the kitchen. After a moment* SUSY *comes in. She looks nervously at* TOM,

77

who is shuddering, his face hidden.)

SUSY: Dad . . .

TOM: (*Muffled*) Get out.

SUSY: Dad?

TOM: (*Roars*) GET OUT!

(SUSY *hurries away.* TOM *gets up. Stands a second. Exits. Lights
fade to blackout.*)

*Lights up: Morning in August a year later. Bright sunshine fills the room.
A six-foot high plant in one corner, smaller ones elsewhere. Feminist
posters on the walls. A wall mirror.*

*MARY opens the door from the hall and comes in. She is dressed for a
wedding, not too formally. Through the open door, loud sounds of a party
down in the pub. Goes into bathroom. Comes back. Examines herself in
the wall mirror. She looks strained and tired.*

After a moment JULIA *comes in.*

MARY: (*Looking at herself*) God, I feel ancient!

JULIA: Well, you're no chicken.

(MARY *winces, then grins*)

MARY: Thanks for the support.

JULIA: D'you need support?

MARY: No . . . no, but I'll be glad when they've all gone.

JULIA: I think they're winding up now.

MARY: Good.

JULIA: Funny . . . that was the first time I'd ever been to a
registry office wedding.

MARY: First time for me too. I'm glad you came.

JULIA: Touch of the sadist! I would have expected Tom to insist
on a church wedding.

MARY: Not up to him. It was Susy's choice. And Nick's. She
wanted the minimum of fuss. I think she would have
preferred a postal wedding, like they do postal divorce now.

JULIA: Tom was on his best behaviour.

MARY: Yes.

JULIA: He wouldn't drink anything except a glass of wine.

MARY: Well, he's driving, isn't he?

JULIA: Yes. Did you talk to him?

78

MARY: No.

JULIA: Didn't you want to?

MARY: It wasn't that.

JULIA: Well?

MARY: He 'cut' me.

JULIA: Huh.

MARY: Don't worry. I'm not bleeding.

JULIA: He's surely not still . . .

MARY: I think he likes to make me feel guilty.

JULIA: You feel guilty! Some hope!

MARY: Actually I do feel guilty.

JULIA: Why should you?

MARY: It's not worth talking about.

JULIA: Sorry.

MARY: I didn't mean to snap.

JULIA: You haven't talked about him for ages.

MARY: There's nothing to talk about.

JULIA: Sorry!

MARY: It's all right.

JULIA: You don't feel anything for him?

MARY: Yes, I feel sorry for him.

> (SUSY *comes up from the pub. Another burst of sound as she opens the door. Closes it.*)

SUSY: We'll be off soon, Mum.

MARY: Are you really going to Southport?

SUSY: Sounds crazy, doesn't it? Our honeymoon: one night of bliss in a hotel in Southport.

JULIA: Honeymoons ain't what they used to be!

MARY: No, they aren't.

SUSY: I'd rather save the money. I told Nick: I can face sharing a life with you but I can't face a night in Southport. But he's determined. Sentimentalist!

MARY: Southport's all right. Quite nice, really.

SUSY: Dad was telling me you used to go there when you were first married.

MARY: Yes . . . when we were first married.

> (*Silence.*)

Susy, I'm not going to be a granny, am I?

79

SUSY: No.

MARY: Oh, good!

SUSY: Not for a while anyway.

MARY: I don't feel quite ready for it yet.

SUSY: American universities seem to have a different attitude to people 'living in sin' on campus, so they advised Nick . . .

MARY: You don't have to apologize for getting married.

SUSY: I was just explaining.

MARY: Well, you don't have to.

SUSY: It was Nick who insisted.

MARY: Was it?

SUSY: Yes.

MARY: What . . . you had reservations?

SUSY: Not about Nick. About marriage.

MARY: I see.

SUSY: And I still feel a slight sense of treason.

MARY: Treason.

SUSY: Yes.

MARY: Why?

SUSY: Oh, just my crazy ideas.

JULIA: Well, I suppose we'd better get to the office.

MARY: Yes.

SUSY: Do you have to go in?

JULIA: 'Fraid so. Show willing. Not that I'll be much use to anyone after all that plonk, eh?

(JULIA *gets her coat.*)

SUSY: Call in and say cheerio.

JULIA: Oh, temptation!

SUSY: Come on.

JULIA: OK.

SUSY: Coming, Mum?

MARY: I'll . . . follow you down.

(SUSY *looks at* MARY.)

SUSY: (*Sharply*) You might have made a bit of an effort, Mum.

MARY: What?

SUSY: With Dad.

MARY: What do you mean?

80

SUSY: You treated him like a stranger.

MARY: Wasn't that what he wanted?

SUSY: You made it obvious it was what you wanted.

MARY: Did I?

SUSY: Yes.

MARY: I thought I was perfectly civil.

SUSY: Yes.

JULIA: She's right, Mary.

(MARY *looks angrily from* SUSY *to* JULIA.)

MARY: Well . . . after all . . . we are strangers now.

SUSY: You don't have to be.

MARY: Too late now anyway.

SUSY: Why? He's still there.

MARY: I've got to get to work.

SUSY: Five minutes wouldn't make any difference, would it?

(MARY *looks uncertainly at* JULIA.)

JULIA: No. Five minutes wouldn't hurt.

(SUSY *goes down to the pub*.)

MARY: Oh, Christ.

JULIA: What?

MARY: Why the hell couldn't she . . .

JULIA: What?

MARY: Suddenly I need a drink. This is ridiculous.

JULIA: Nervous?

MARY: I feel embarrassed.

JULIA: 'Weak at the knees'?

MARY: Christ, Julia, I shouldn't tell you anything!

JULIA: Don't worry about the office. There's no rush. And I can always cover for you.

MARY: Thanks.

JULIA: Get yourself a large drink.

(MARY *quickly goes to the kitchen*. JULIA *leaves quickly. After a moment* SUSY *comes in with* TOM. TOM *stops her*.)

TOM: Hang on . . . here . . . (*Gives her an envelope*.) I didn't want to flash that down there.

SUSY: What is it?

TOM: Prezzy.

SUSY: You've already given us a present.

TOM: That's for you, not both of you.

SUSY: No, Dad.

TOM: Don't say anything to Nick, now.

SUSY: Secrets . . . from my husband?

TOM: (*Grins.*) There's always a few secrets. Anyway, you never know . . . it's always handy, having a few quid in reserve.

SUSY: But can you afford it?

TOM: Yes, I'm loaded. The cab's a goldmine. I'm never off the road. Keeps me out of trouble!

SUSY: Well, thanks. We were a bit short.

TOM: Remember, it's for you.

(MARY *has appeared at the kitchen door but stays there.*)

SUSY: All right.

TOM: Keep in touch.

SUSY: I will!

(SUSY *embraces* TOM *emotionally.* TOM *looks over her shoulder and sees* MARY. MARY *comes toward them, embarrassed.*)

TOM: Send me a card from Southport.

SUSY: Oh, sure! Bye, Dad.

TOM: Are you going?

SUSY: Yes, have to fly. Bye, Mum.

(SUSY *kisses* MARY.)

MARY: Bye, love. Love to Nick.

(SUSY *leaves.*)

TOM: Where's Julia?

MARY: She's just gone.

TOM: What . . . gone to work?

MARY: Yes. I'll have to go in a few minutes.

TOM: Oh. I see. Well . . . I'm sorry I missed her.

MARY: She had to dash.

TOM: Didn't have a chance to say goodbye.

MARY: Well, we hardly had a chance to say hello, did we?

TOM: Hello.

MARY: Was that your car by the pub?

TOM: My car . . . and my livelihood.

MARY: How long have you been driving a cab?

TOM: Over six months now.

MARY: Do you enjoy it?

TOM: It's all right. At least I'm my own boss.

MARY: Fancy a beer?

TOM: I'd love one.

(MARY *goes to the kitchen.* TOM *glances at a poster.* MARY *returns with a beer for* TOM *and a glass of wine.*)

MARY: Cheers.

TOM: Cheers.

(MARY *perches on a cushion on the floor. Looks up at* TOM, *standing awkwardly.*)

MARY: Have a seat.

TOM: Haven't you got any chairs yet?

MARY: Only in the kitchen. It's more comfortable to sprawl.

(TOM *sits gingerly.*)

TOM: Haven't got cockroaches, have you?

MARY: No, just spiders and beetles.

TOM: How long have you er . . . known Susy was getting married?

MARY: Since I got the invite.

TOM: Same here!

(*They laugh.*)

(*Looking around*) You've done yourself proud here, Mary.

MARY: I like it.

TOM: Bit different from mine . . .

MARY: What's your place like?

TOM: Like a cell belonging to a very dirty monk.

MARY: You haven't changed!

TOM: 'Fraid not.

MARY: So . . . Susy's married.

TOM: Yup.

MARY: I'm glad.

TOM: That your verdict?

MARY: No . . .

TOM: It's not the end of the story.

MARY: I know.

TOM: And it's certainly not the beginning.

MARY: What is it then?

TOM: Just an episode.

MARY: You sound very cynical.

83

TOM: Just realistic. It might work for her. It might not. But she's got to try it and find out.

MARY: She didn't have to try it.

TOM: She wanted to.

MARY: Did she discuss it with you?

TOM: You're joking!

(TOM *drinks his beer, laughing*.)

MARY: Nick is really her first boyfriend, isn't he?

TOM: Yeah.

MARY: First serious boyfriend, I mean.

TOM: Yeah.

MARY: I didn't expect her to follow in our footsteps . . .

TOM: Well, no . . . not . . . all the way.

(MARY *takes his glass*.)

MARY: Another?

TOM: Yes, ta.

(MARY *refills the drinks*.)

MARY: Cheers.

TOM: I knew she was keen on Nick, of course, but I wasn't really expecting wedding bells . . . not just yet, anyway.

MARY: What wedding bells?

TOM: She told me that she didn't want a white wedding and all that hypocrisy.

MARY: Sounds like our girl!

TOM: Anyway, she's not a Catholic. Not really. Not even a lapsed Catholic, really.

MARY: Neither am I . . . really.

TOM: I'm the only one left.

MARY: You still practise. . . ?

TOM: Oh aye. More than ever. Means more to me now than it ever did.

MARY: Why's that?

TOM: I dunno. Age, I suppose.

MARY: Tom, you're only 42.

TOM: Well into the second half.

MARY: In a way, I envy you your faith.

TOM: Do you?

MARY: Yes.

TOM: Why?

MARY: Well . . . in a way . . . I feel as if I've spent my life skimming the surface . . . I've made do with, oh, superficial things. You *can't* do that.

TOM: (*Smiles.*) Can't I?

MARY: No, you always have to drill deeper and deeper and deeper. I'm not saying it makes for happiness. In fact I know it makes for the opposite. I know that you've had a kind of . . . inner pressure which I never used to understand.

TOM: You understand it now?

MARY: I think so. And I envy you it.

TOM: Wish I understood it! I never knew how to handle it, but . . . well, as you get a bit older, you learn ways . . .

MARY: What ways?

TOM: Work, mainly. Drink, sometimes. Distractions . . . (*They drink.*)

MARY: When I said that I was glad Susy was married, I think what I meant was . . . I was glad not to feel responsible for her any more.

TOM: I haven't felt responsible for her since she was 18.

MARY: You can't just switch off at an age on the calendar.

TOM: But . . . you think you can switch off once they get married?

MARY: It must lessen your responsibility as a parent, mustn't it?

TOM: Once you have kids you've given hostages to life . . . for life.

MARY: Do you think we let her down?

TOM: What . . . by separating?

MARY: Or before?

TOM: Who can say?

MARY: Oh, you're a real friend in need, Tom.

TOM: Am I?

MARY: You're really easing my conscience.

TOM: You feel guilty, do you? About Susy?

MARY: I can't help it.

TOM: Susy couldn't give a damn.

MARY: About me?

TOM: About your guilt, or mine.

MARY: Do you feel guilty then?

TOM: Every good Catholic has guilt in his bloodstream.

MARY: I couldn't help wondering if she rushed into an early marriage because of our example—

TOM: Not much of an example.

MARY: Or even because we failed.

TOM: Look, Mary, we're not at the centre of Susy's life any more. From now on her family is Nick.

MARY: She's still our daughter . . . as you said . . . a hostage for life.

TOM: We brought her into the world, so we'll always be on call. We owe her that. But as far as she's concerned we're on the margins of her life. We might see her at birthdays, or Christmas . . . or weddings and funerals . . . but you and me are no longer central. We haven't been central for years. (MARY's *eyes are wet.* TOM *moves closer to her.*) You shouldn't feel any guilt. It was inevitable. She's a good girl. She's fine. She's really happy. You've no reason to feel guilty. (MARY's *eyes are streaming. She hides her face.* TOM *touches her shoulder.*) Or are you weeping for your lost child? Your lost daughter? (TOM *hugs* MARY.) Go on, have a good cry. It's a mother's privilege.

MARY: I'm not crying for Susy . . .

TOM: What?

MARY: (*Breaking*) I'm crying for us! (*Gasps, struggles for control.*) For you and me. (TOM *looks away.* MARY *gets up, stumbles, goes to bathroom.*) I'm sorry . . . I didn't mean that . . . I just . . . (MARY *goes into the bathroom.* TOM *stands.*)

TOM: Mary? (*Hesitates.*) Mary. . . ? (MARY *comes back, wiping her eyes.*)

MARY: I'm sorry about that.

TOM: Why were you crying for us?

MARY: It was nothing.

TOM: Does it still hurt?

MARY: No. Well . . . sometimes. How about you?

TOM: Yes. It still hurts. Sometimes. At least I've got the consolation of knowing I got what I asked for. I brought it on myself.

MARY: We got out of our depth.

TOM: How?

MARY: It's strange. You can live quite happily, quite cosily, at the shallow end without even realizing it, and then you take a few short steps and suddenly you're in the deep end and you're drowning.

TOM: Oh, well . . . (*Breezy*) We learnt to swim, didn't we?

MARY: I'm not that much of a swimmer but I'm learning. Why were you so distant . . . at the wedding?

TOM: Why were you?

MARY: Self-protection.

TOM: Oh. You don't have to protect yourself against me, love, do you?

(MARY *looks at* TOM, *hesitates*.)

MARY: What do you think?

(TOM *takes* MARY *in his arms. Blackout.*)

Lights up: Evening of the same day.

TOM, *open-shirted, lies asleep on the cushions. After a moment* MARY *comes from the kitchen, carrying a glass of water. Puts on a tape: Cat Stevens's 'My Lady D'Arbanville'. Sits by* TOM *so as not to disturb him. Traces a finger lightly over his face. He opens his eyes. Smiles. Moves to kiss* MARY *but she stops him.*

MARY: I've been scrutinizing you for over half an hour.

TOM: Did you come to any conclusion?

MARY: I love you . . . even if I can't live with you.

TOM: Who says you can't?

MARY: Me.

TOM: Oh.

MARY: You don't want to live with me, do you?

TOM: No.

MARY: It doesn't stop me loving you.

TOM: More than anyone else in the world?

87

MARY: Yes.

TOM: Oh, who are all the others?

MARY: Well, there's Susy . . . and Julia . . . and . . .

TOM: And Co.

MARY: Co.?

TOM: That's how I'll think of it: Susy, Julia and Co. The other people you love.

MARY: How's your love life?

TOM: Beautiful . . . at this moment.

MARY: Do you have lots of . . . friends?

TOM: I don't have friends, I have passengers. (*Sips his drink. Smiles.*)

It's all pretty tatty, isn't it?

MARY: Is it?

TOM: It never was with you.

MARY: If the two of us could just climb into this moment and stay there . . .

TOM: Are you suggesting a suicide pact?

MARY: No.

TOM: It's against my religious principles.

MARY: When we were teenagers we used to go on like that. Remember?

TOM: (*Laughs.*) Yes. 'Would you kill yourself if I was dying?'

MARY: I said I would.

TOM: So did I.

MARY: I never said that to anyone else, anyway.

TOM: Nor did I.

(MARY *kisses* TOM.)

MARY: Oh, Christ.

TOM: Don't go all weepy on me again.

MARY: Why not? It worked last time.

TOM: Oh, cheeky!

(*They wrestle for a moment, laughing.*)

MARY: I'll cry if I feel like crying.

TOM: You'll unman me.

MARY: I like you unmanned.

(MARY *sips the water, gives* TOM *a sip.*)

There's something I ought to tell you.

TOM: What?

MARY: I don't know whether I should tell you, though.

TOM: Why not?

MARY: You'll leave me.

TOM: What is it? Have you got another bloke in the kitchen?

MARY: No.

TOM: Look, Mary, I know we've both got other people . . .
relationships, whatever you like . . . at least I have and I
take it you have . . . So you might as well tell me.

MARY: You won't walk out?

TOM: Tell me.

MARY: You left your car on a double yellow line.

TOM: Let them tow it away!
(*They embrace, laughing.*)

Lights change: Moonlight.
    MARY *lies on the cushions, asleep.* TOM *comes on with a blanket, and
places it over her. He kneels nearby, saying a Hail Mary.*

TOM: Hail Mary, full of grace, the Lord is with Thee, and
blessed art Thou among women . . .
(*Lights fade to blackout.*)

Lights up: The following morning. Empty room.
    MARY *comes in from the kitchen, wearing a dressing-gown, and
carrying a tray with a teapot and cups. Puts this down by the cushions.*
TOM *comes after her, in shirtsleeves, from bathroom. They sit.* MARY *pours
tea.*

TOM: Hey, I was thinking . . . remember the time I ordered that
white sports car?

MARY: You denied it!

TOM: Yeah.

MARY: The man brought it to the house. I didn't know what to
say!
(*They laugh.*)

TOM: What I did feel guilty about . . . was the time I marched
into the office and shouted at Bob Reece.

MARY: I was the talk of the typing pool for ages. They've felt let down ever since.

TOM: I think that was the point when I really blew it, wasn't it?

MARY: Well, you did corner him in the pub and invite him to come and stay at our house.

TOM: Oh, Jeez, I'd forgotten that!

MARY: He wouldn't go into the pub for weeks after that.

TOM: Christ.

MARY: Terrified of meeting you.

TOM: Did anything develop . . . with you and him?

MARY: No . . . there was nothing . . . just . . .

TOM: Are you still working with him?

MARY: No, he transferred to Southampton.

TOM: Oh, I see . . . that's why nothing developed.

MARY: Tom, I told you. I never did fancy Bob Reece. Did anything develop between you and that girl in Susy's flat?

TOM: Linda?

MARY: Yes, that's right. Linda.

TOM: Oh, I blew the whistle on her.

MARY: Oh, aye.

TOM: I did. She was too demanding. Ask Susy.

MARY: Susy was involved, eh?

TOM: She knew I was feeling down.

MARY: My daughter procuring for her father!

TOM: Don't imagine it was only Linda, like . . .

MARY: I bet you had a ball in that commune!

TOM: Well . . . I didn't go short, like!

MARY: Remember the time you bought all that sexy underwear?

TOM: Oh, aye.

MARY: I was cringing with embarrassment in the shop.

TOM: You looked good in it, though.

MARY: Hmmmm.

TOM: Haven't got it here, have you? Haven't got it handy?

MARY: After last night I doubt if you'd be up to it.

TOM: Try me.

MARY: Didn't you say you had plans for today?

TOM: Yeah, the Reds are at home today.

MARY: Did you renew your season ticket?

TOM: Yeah.

MARY: Good.

TOM: But I'm not going today.

MARY: Why not?

TOM: D'you want me to go?

MARY: Only if you want . . .

TOM: Any more tea?

(MARY *pours tea*.)

MARY: I don't want you to go to the match.

TOM: What I'd like is just to relax today . . . and then go out about seven, have a few jars and then a nice meal.

MARY: I thought you said tonight was the busiest night of the week with the cab?

TOM: It is.

MARY: Maybe we should go out tomorrow night?

TOM: More fun on a Saturday night.

MARY: Well, as it happens . . .

TOM: What?

MARY: Nothing.

TOM: Come on . . . we said no secrets.

MARY: I've got a date.

TOM: A date?

MARY: Yes.

TOM: I should have realized . . . Saturday night.

MARY: I'll cancel it.

TOM: No.

MARY: Why not?

TOM: It's not fair on . . . whoever it is.

MARY: It's someone I met at work. I've been out with him two or three times . . .

TOM: You don't have to explain.

MARY: I wanted to. I'll cancel it. (*Goes to phone, dials*.) Francis? Look, I'm sorry, but I just can't make it tonight. Yes, all right. Maybe next week. See you on Monday. Have a nice weekend. (*Hangs up*.) A nice weekend. He's divorced. Sees his children on Sundays. He's a wreck for days afterwards.

TOM: Tough.

(MARY *stands behind* TOM *and puts her arms round his shoulders*.)

91

MARY: All right?

TOM: Yeah. Sure about tonight?

MARY: We'll have a night to remember.

(TOM *stands, kisses* MARY, *and smiles.*)

TOM: We'll do that.

(TOM *goes to the bathroom.* MARY *begins gathering the things on the tray. Lights fade to blackout.*)

Lights up: That evening. About seven.

TOM *comes from the kitchen, carrying a drink. He is fixing his tie. Looks quite spruce for the night out. Picks up his coat and puts it on. Sits comfortably on the cushions.*

After a moment MARY *comes in from the bathroom wearing a short slip. Looks glamorous.* TOM *whistles and drums his feet.* MARY *takes a hairbrush from a drawer.*

MARY: I won't be two minutes.

TOM: I don't know why we're going out!

MARY: What?

TOM: I think I'd rather stay in!

(MARY *takes a puff on his cigarette.*)

MARY: I've given up but tonight's a special night.

(TOM *draws her down. She pulls back.*)

Tom . . .

TOM: You know, when I told people I was in love with my wife they used to look at me as if I was crazy.

MARY: Don't go all cynical on me.

TOM: I'm not being cynical. Am I being sentimental?

MARY: Do you still love your wife?

TOM: Yes.

MARY: And we're going to be friends?

TOM: Friends . . . and lovers.

(MARY *smiles, pecks him on the lips, goes into bathroom. Phone rings.* TOM *answers it.*)

Hello. Yes, that's the number. My name's Tom, if you want to know. Who are you? Allan? Yes, she's here. (*Calls*) Mary, phone.

(MARY *comes in.*)

MARY: Who is it?

TOM: Some bloke. Allan.

(TOM *leaves the phone and sits.*)

MARY *(Startled)* Allan? (*Takes the phone.*) Hello? Allan? Where are you? Here? I thought you were staying in London over the weekend? But . . . No, I'll bet you couldn't. No, I can't. I'm sorry. I really can't. Impossible. (*Looks at* TOM.) My husband, actually. Yes. I'll explain. No, not tomorrow. Give me a ring on Monday. Yes, yes, we will. Oh, don't fret! Bye. (*Puts the phone down. Looks at* TOM. *Awkward*) That was—

TOM: Allan.

MARY: Yes. Won't be a sec.

(MARY *goes toward the bathroom. As she does so, the phone rings again.* TOM *gets up quickly and takes it.* MARY *turns back.*)

TOM: Allan.

MARY: Damn.

(TOM *hands the phone to her.*)

Hello? What? No, it's nothing to do with that. I know you were drunk. It's just that I've arranged to go out . . . yes, now, if you'll let me. How could I know you'd rush back? All right. Ring me tomorrow. No, not tonight. I . . . (*Glances at* TOM.) I don't know. Maybe. Leave it till tomorrow. Tomorrow afternoon. Yes, you go and get drunk now. (*Hangs up.*) God! He said he'd be in London for the weekend and now he . . . Allan is a marketing consultant. He travels around a lot. I've known him a few months and he—

(TOM *puts his finger to his mouth and* MARY *stops. Smiles.*) Sorry.

(TOM *smiles back.* MARY *goes to the bathroom to put on her dress.* TOM *takes a look round the flat. Goes to the door. Looks back. Quietly leaves.* MARY *comes back wearing her dress.*)

How do I look? (*Realizes he's not in the room.*) Tom? (*Glances into the kitchen and hall.*) Tom?

(*Realizes he has gone. Comes back. Picks up a beer can and glass that he has left. Holds it for a second. Stands, steps across the cushions, spilling a little of the drink. Goes out to the kitchen. Music: 'Only you', the Platters.*)

(*Blackout.*)